The Vanishing

Ron Mueller

❧ The Vanishing ☙

<u>Fiction Series</u>
The Alex Evercrest Series
The River Front
The Girl on The Grill
Missing
Maggot
Racist
Votive Candles
Windy City
Country Road
Pool of Blood
Sins of the Daughter
Body Parts
The Skull Collector
The Vanishing
The Shadow Fighter
Moonshine
Grief's Trajectory
The Magic Touch
Northern Lights
Alex Evercrest Heroine
Alex Evercrest Collection Two
New Direction
Disruption
A Family Affair
The St. Lebuinnus Church Murder

A Brian O'Neil Novel
Hawaiian Phoenix
Moon Curser
Death Broker

The Problem Solver Series
Solutions
Drug Lords
Border Crosser
The Problem Solver Collection

<u>The Taelo Series</u>
Taelo: The Early Years
Taelo: The Golden Feather
Taelo: Journey of Discovery
Taelo: Dangerous Passage
Taelo: Condor Clan Slingers
Taelo: Circumvention
Taelo: The Journey of Sages
Taelo: Collection
Taelo: Future Leaders Journey

<u>A Taelo Story:</u>
White Swan and Quiet Pheasant
The Child's Name
Floating Cloud
Quiet Rabbit
Busy Bee
Little Otter & Talking Wren
Broken Spear
Burley Bear & Meadow Flower
Taelo Story Collection

<u>Science Fiction</u>

The Savitar Series:
Journey's End
Savitar
Confluence
Savitar Series Collection

Bram Nielson Series
The Fold
The Message
Fold Wormhole
Negative Fold
Ripples in Time
Bram Nielson Collection

<u>Single Science Fiction Books:</u>
Current Past and Future
The Event
The Door
Viajante 7

❧ The Vanishing ☙
By: *Ron Mueller*

Around the World Publishing LLC
Cincinnati, Ohio

Ron Mueller

ISBN 13: 978-1-68223-990-2

Distributed by Ingram
Cover Picture by: Sidorov Ruslan @ShutterStock
Cover Design by: Ron Mueller

The Vanishing

1 Comacho

A red bandana hugged the head of the person handing a small package to the person who in turn was passing a hand full of cash back to his other hand. This was a scene being repeated in numerous dark corners or alleys throughout the city. Business was booming and Comacho controlled a lucrative part of the drug distribution business. He was not the biggest distributor. He was one of the toughest and in control of his distribution area, and he was raking in the money. He purposely kept a low profile and maintained good relations with his competitors by agreeing to the territory in which he distributed, and he gave a small cut of the take to keep the good relations greased. His adversaries also were very aware of his ruthlessness.

He knew he was destined to go to hell. He figured he might be able to pal around with the Devil. He planned to continue to be ruthless and to control those who worked for him. He had grown up as one of the Reds and had learned that strength and ruthlessness were the ingredients that let one survive in the harsh environment that he had been raised in.

He had no patience with those who hesitated to do as he commanded. He had personally shot and killed more than a dozen men and women. Yes women! They demanded equal treatment, and he gladly gave it to them. He had no patience for insubordination. When he ordered something, he expected immediate follow-through, and he usually got it.

There were two ways he handled those he decided to eliminate.

Regular offenders who would not pay out or distributors that encroached on his territory were taken care of by his hirelings.

For those more egregious offenders he had a special ceremony that he personally orchestrated. He would have a fifty-gallon barrel filled three quarters of the way with a chemical that was heavy on lye, and he would have his nude victim placed feet first into the barrel. Then he would ask the screaming individual to ask him to shoot and kill them. When they asked him to shoot, he would but he would shoot that person in the arm. Then he would ask the screaming individual to tell him where he should shoot. Often the request was in the head, sometimes through the heart. But he would not do it until he made the person say, "Please shoot me in the ---." Often the legs of the individual would give out and he had to be held in the vertical position.

Once the individual was dead, he left the area after giving instructions to sink the body into the drum and then seal it.

The drum was filled to the very brim before sealing it so it would sink like a rock. He had the drum taken out to sea and ensured it would sink by adding additional weight to it.

Only one woman had suffered that fate. She was an assassin hired by a competitor drug dealer. She had been the toughest of the twelve that had stood in the barrel. When he asked her where he should shoot her, she had screamed "put the bullet in your head" and she had then she crouched down into the barrel and put her head under the chemical bath.

He had been amazed by her toughness she had not started to scream when placed into the barrel! He almost regretted that she had tried to kill him. He figured she might have been his soul mate. A vile soul mate from hell. "Oh, well," he laughed as he thought about the Devil sending him a message.

He decided to kill the drug dealer that had hired her, to see if he would be as tough as she had been. He was not. He cried and screamed like a baby.

Ironically, the word got out about his having eliminated the female assassin and the drug dealer and he was charged with murder. He of course pleaded innocent. The problem for the prosecutor was that he did not have a body and was operating on hearsay. His lawyer and the prosecutor reached an agreement that if he left the state the case would be dropped.

He set up his second in command to run the drug distribution business. He wanted thirty per cent of the take to be sent to an offshore account.

He had no plans to stop distributing so he looked around to see where in the country he would set himself up.

He figured he needed to find a low-profile location but one that was well positioned geographically in the drug trade.

He looked north to Seattle and decided that it was not well located.

He looked to Chicago but realized that the battle between the Mafia and the Mexican cartels would put him in the middle between two powerful and deadly groups. That situation eliminated Chicago.

New York City was out because of the state's focus on rooting out drug distributors. It would make it hard to carve out distribution territory.

He went down the list of the large cities in the east and eliminated all of them.

He looked at the US map and realized that one central point in the drug distribution was the city that had been described by one New Yorker as, "the sleepy little city by the Ohio River." He moved the arrow on the screen and made a circle around Cincinnati.

He bought a one-way first-class plane ticket to Cincinnati.

He had his Mercedes-Benz SL Cabriolet driven there so that he would have his favorite car to use.

He spent a few days in Cincinnati in a luxury downtown hotel suite while he explored the city on foot. He walked the Ohio Riverfront Park. He located the police station and walked all around that area.

He found the place he was looking for. It was a bar about three blocks away from the police station. He walked in and asked the current owner what he wanted for the place.

The owner asked why he would want a place that did not do much business. He said that he was ready to sell but didn't want to unload a dying bar. He gave a price of what he thought the building and property was worth and said that he currently was breaking even on the business. He asked again why he would want to buy the business.

Camacho replied that it seemed to be located in a place close to the downtown area but out of the beaten path. He agreed to the asking price but wanted six months' time before he needed to make the payment.

He then asked who the regular customers happened to be and was not surprised to learn that there were several cops that frequented the place. He hoped that one of them would be open to a little extra cash for inside information about what was coming down. He also needed to make sure the regular cops were willing to look the other way to the traffic of distributors that might be entering and leaving the bar.

He made it a point to be friendly with all of the cops that came in and slowly figured out which one was most likely to be susceptible to making a lucrative arrangement and would agree to be an inside informant.

When that policeman's bar bill began to build up, he made his proposal. The policeman thought he was a great bargainer and bargained for free drinks as a part of such an arrangement. Comacho figured that a bottle of booze a week was a very cheap bribe and he added that if he got the information that he requested he would sweeten the arrangement. He figured that he could keep the monetary honey at a low level.

His early requests were simple and information he could get himself, but it provided a way to get the informant relaxed and willing to share information. The first thing he asked about was the number of high schools inside the two seventy-five loop. He figured the roughly twenty-five that he got an address for would be about the right number to set up a lucrative and low-key drug distribution network.

It was time to set up a small local distribution organization. He reached back to his L.A. network and got the names of three individuals that he could hire. One was located in Cincinnati; one was from L.A. who had worked for him there and one was from the Columbus area. He figured the mix would give him a small group that had the moxie to run the operation. He hired the three and assigned them the role of recruiting drug distributors at each of the high schools and distributing the drugs to them.

He gave them the profile of a good high school drug distributor. The individual had to be a person that demonstrated being a leader but who was either a loner or an individual who bullied others.

It could be a female but most often would probably be a male. He or she would stand out during the morning when school started and during the end of the day rush out of the school. He or she could be of any race. The poorer the better. However, they could not be on any drugs to be a distributor.

The individual would be given a starting bonus and initially five percent of the sales income.

He let the three who would be doing the recruiting know that they would each get five percent of the drugs their high school distributors sold so they should make sure to coach them and give them some additional rewards like free meals or rides to social events. In other words, set up a positive relationship with these young distributors. Finally, they should be setting up the next person to take the place of a high schooler that was graduating.

Setting up the distribution network and getting a local drug production facility established took him about six months. He was lucky and found an abandoned fire station just across town that he was able to lease. He imported a druggist from L.A. and set him up in the station. He funded the operation but stayed well away from what he figured was a group of druggies making more drugs.

He was able to buy a large home with several acres on the east side of the city that was only about fifteen minutes from the bar where he would have his operational office.

He felt good about the transition. Cincinnati did not have the nightlife that was available in L.A., but it featured a variety of engaging theatrical plays, orchestra performances, boating on nearby lakes and on the Ohio River. He figured he would enjoy a quieter lifestyle and become more active outdoors.

<u>2 *The Vanishing*</u>

*T*he hallway was a maze of students weaving around each other, talking in small groups, or yelling to friends. There were also confrontations between some students and consistently three bullies would corner some person but most often some young female that they would harass.

Jesse navigated his way down the crowded hall as he hastened to make it to his next class. He had just escaped another scrimmage with these three bullies who were his nemesis. He was being hounded because he had interceded when the three had cornered a reluctant female student. The three were recognized throughout the school as bullies. He also suspected them of being the school's drug suppliers. He was certain they were connected to the Red Bandana gang that controlled the drug distribution in the area. This worried him because he knew that the gang was violent and would corner a person when they were alone.

It was Saturday morning, and he was on the way to buy a new pair of basketball shoes. He spotted a young woman being harassed.

He should have minded his own business, but she was getting attacked by these three mean looking dudes wearing red bandanas. He shouted at them to stop and when they turned to respond to him the lady dashed away.

He took off but they caught up with him. When they caught up with him, he realized they were the three bullies that often pushed him around at school. He knew he was in big trouble.

They began pounding on him and said they were going to beat him to death. He fought as best as he could, but he took a brutal beating. It only stopped when a police car came driving by and turned on its red lights.

He used that moment, like the young woman, to dash away but he heard one of the bully's shout at him that they were not through with him or anyone else in his family.

The image of his sister came to his mind. His sister, April, was only fifteen and was a freshman. She was excited about beginning high school. She was doing well in her classes, was a junior varsity cheer leader and had a minor role in one of the theatrical school plays.

He adored April. He figured if he vanished from the scene, the three hoods would move on, and she would be alright. This was all he could think of as he ran seemingly in a random direction.

That had been earlier in a grey cloud covered day that deteriorated into a continuous drizzle that had seemed determined to make him cold and miserable. His sweatshirt was soaked and the only reason he kept it on was because even in the wet condition it was keeping him warm.

He pulled his hood tight trying to keep the drizzle out. The day had faded into a night as dark as the thoughts in his mind. He found himself walking eastward but he had no clue where he was going. The blood had stopped running from his nose and the drizzle seemed to be keeping it moistened. His other cuts had all crusted over. He was a mess. He would need to find a place where he could wash up so he would be somewhat presentable. He felt lucky to have escaped alive.

The beating had been almost eight hours ago. The rumble in his stomach gave him a blunt unadulterated reality check about his current situation. He was wet, he was hungry, and he had no place to stop to get some sleep.

He had just made the basketball team and that morning he had emptied his money box so he could buy a new pair of Nike basketball shoes. That money was in his backpack. The idea of buying the Nike shoes was now history. That money had to last until he could get to wherever he was going, and until he got paid for the job, a job that he knew he needed to get.

He wondered if he had enough cash to carry him through until he had a job and a first paycheck. He thought about how his mother stretched her paycheck to make sure she always had food for the family. She always bought fifty-pound bags of rice and beans, large jars of peanut butter, of strawberry jam and grape jelly, and day-old loaves of bread. She made a point of letting him and April know that chicken, ham, and any other meat was a treat and would be cooked sparingly.

He figured that he would have to copy what she did when shopping so he could stretch the money he had in the backpack.

He looked ahead and saw a large honeysuckle bush growing under a railway overpass. He crawled under it and got as close to the trunk of the bush as possible and made himself as comfortable as he could. He would have liked to take off his wet sweatshirt, but the night was already cold to him. He hoped that it would be sunny the next day so he could dry off.

He felt like death warmed over, was miserable but he finally fell asleep.

The morning sun woke him up and the clear blue cloudless sky gave his down feelings a lift. He took off his sweatshirt and hung it from his backpack. His long sleeve shirt was damp to the touch, but it soon dried off as he walked.

He was on one of the smaller highways going east across Ohio. The occasional car or pickup went by, but none stopped to offer him a ride. As a Black man he did not expect to get picked up. He took long strides and kept walking.

Just about the time he was about to give up on getting to somewhere where he could get something to eat, he came up over a hill and saw that down in the valley, there was a small one street village hugging the banks of a small river. Tall old oaks and maples provided a shading canopy for most of the buildings in town. They appeared to be the barrier that kept the weeping willows along the river at bay. As he approached the town, it was as if he had stepped back in time. He half expected to see gunslingers and horses.

He saw only one store that had a sign advertising that they were a hardware and grocery. He entered and was greeted by an older lady sitting on a tall stool who asked him how she could be of help.

He asked if she had any sandwiches or something that he could have for a late breakfast. She led the way to the back of the store where there was a large coffee pot, a microwave and small freezer that had a variety of sandwiches and other microwaveable offerings.

She let him know that a cup of coffee and any one selection from the freezer was five dollars.

After looking over the selection he chose a mac and cheese package because it was the largest amount of food.

After wolfing down the food he walked around the small grocery section and selected a two-pound bag of rice and a large bag of dry black beans. He then found a small metal pan that he figured he would use to cook with. Finally, he picked up a large bottle of water.

He took everything to the counter where, as his selection was being rung up, the lady asked where he was going.

He answered that he was not sure but somewhere along the East Coast.

She smiled and let him know that in the next town he would be able to catch a bus. She then let him know that breakfast was on her and wished him good luck.

He thanked her for being so kind and then paid her with some of his precious cash.

He then went on his way. Now he was thinking about where on the East Coast he would go, and he wondered if he had enough money to buy the ticket and still have enough left over so he could last until he landed a job.

In the next town he located the bus station. He was surprised that he could go to almost anywhere along the East Coast for about one hundred dollars.

He felt a sense of relief that he would have enough money left over for food, but he would need to figure out where to sleep at night. He was sure that he would not be able to stay in any hotel or motel.

After considering the cities along the coast, he chose Virginia Beach as the place that he would try to establish himself. He was not at all sure why he had selected it, but it seemed to be the halfway point between going north or going south.

The bus ride gave him time to get some sleep, think through what he would do so he could feed himself and where he might be able to find a place where he could sleep.

He figured he would have to locate a homeless shelter and hope that he would get the help he needed to find a job and an affordable place to live.

The bus arrived early in the morning. Once again, his stomach was growling. He walked out of the bus station and looked around. He saw an old Black guy pushing a cart filled with bottles and tin cans.

He walked over to him and asked if he knew where a person could get something to eat at no cost.

The old guy looked at him and told him he was too young to become a beggar and should get a job.

Jesse nodded and asked him where he might find a job.

The old guy smiled and said that he should go to the Mayfair Home of Hope where he could get a good meal and while he was there, he should see if they could point him to a job. He added that it would not be a job being the president of some company, but it would let him make enough to let him eat. He pointed at his cart and said that his other option was to collect bottles and cans and take them to the recycling center where he would get about two cents per bottle and a penny a can. He added that he covered the territory for blocks around and would fight him off.

Jesse thanked him for the information and asked for directions to the Home of Hope.

The old man pointed in the direction opposite to the one he was going and said that it was about seven blocks. He said good luck and continued on his way.

Jesse took up a brisk walk and he soon saw the sign outside a building that looked like it might once have been an apartment building.

He read the sign on the outside of the building that said it gave food, comfort, and the opportunity to start anew.

He figured that he qualified and that he was certainly starting new.

He walked up the steps and entered.

He was greeted by a gray bearded person that looked like an anemic Santa Claus. He was asked what he needed.

Jesse let it all flow out, "something to eat, a place to sleep and a job."

The old guy said that he was in luck and would be able to get a tray of food before the breakfast line closed to get ready for the noon meal. He told Jesse to get his tray of food and while he was eating a social worker would come out to ask him a few questions.

Jessi went in, grabbed a tray, and went down the line.

There was only one server who smiled and put huge helpings on the tray. He commented that normally he should not expect so much but it had been a slow morning. The server put two apples and two bananas on the counter and said he should take them as well.

Jessi could hardly carry the tray to the nearest table. He looked around and realized he was one of five people in the cafeteria.

He was famished and dug in. The scrambled eggs, the three patties of sausage, and a large blue berry muffin disappeared. He went over to a large coffee pot and poured himself a cup and put in three creamers and carried it back to his table to finish a sugar covered cake donut. He planned to eat the bananas and apples later.

An older Black woman approached and introduced herself as Renee and let him know that she was a registered nurse and psychologist, and she had a few questions to ask him.

Jesse nodded and waited for the questions.

The first question was about his age, then what level of education he had and then what job experience he had.

She reacted to his age and said that he looked older than eighteen. Then she asked why he had not finished high school.

Jesse said that he had to run because he had crossed wires with the local drug dealer, and they had threatened to kill him and had almost succeed. He opened his shirt to show the bruises that were now turning yellow.

He then listened as Renee said that he was in luck, and she would be able to take him in and get him an interview at a local restaurant as a bus boy. The pay would not be enough to enable him to rent a room somewhere so he might need to get a second job. However, he would have a couple months to get the second job and to find a place to live.

She asked if he wanted to finish getting his high school diploma.

Jesse said getting a high school diploma would be great and would give him the chance to try and go on to college.

Renee smiled and said that she liked his attitude and said that he would be shown to his room, and he should get oriented. She added that there would be no cooking in the room. If he had a hot plate, he should not think about using it.

She told him that he should be ready to go at eight the next morning. She was going to make a couple of calls and get a job interview lined up.

Once in his room, he got oriented. It had a shower, a bar of soap, and some towels. He decided to take a shower and wash his t-shirt, drawers and socks and put them in the sunlight to dry. He wrapped the towel around his waist and lay down on the bed. The mattress was a hard one that he thought was just what he needed.

He went to sleep wondering how he would wake up to get to breakfast and be ready by eight.

A blasting horn in the hallway at six in the morning brough him wide awake. He now knew that he would not have to buy an alarm clock.

He got up and went to the sink, opened the medicine cabinet, and found a comb, a toothbrush, and a tube of toothpaste. He brushed his teeth, spruce up, got dressed in his still damp clothes and went down the stairs to the cafeteria.

By six thirty he had a tray in hand and went down the breakfast line and selected the over easy eggs, some sausage, two pieces of toast and two patties of butter. He added a carton of milk and took a banana. He looked around and realized he was one of the first people in the cafeteria.

Renee came over to his table and gave him a card with the person at the restaurant that would be expecting him, and that the restaurant was a twelve-block walk.

Jesse asked for the directions and Renee handed him a piece of paper with a hand drawn map on it.

He thanked her for getting him an interview so quickly. He added that he hoped to come back and let her know that he had a job.

He left right after breakfast and after a brisk walk arrived thirty minutes early. He let the breakfast host know he had come for a job interview.

He was asked to wait at the entrance. He watched the people arriving and realized he was definitely in a white neighborhood.

The manager came out and led him to a table in the back corner where he offered him something to drink.

He said that the water would be fine.

The grey-haired white manager appeared to him to be in his late forties or maybe early fifties. He was clearly overweight and seemed out of shape.

He asked a few questions and then asked him to sign a paper that would let the restaurant to check his background. He then offered a busboys job, one meal each day, the minimum hourly rate of pay plus a share of the tips.

Jesse accepted and asked when he could begin.

The manager replied that it could be immediately and asked Jesse to follow him.

3 *Cincinnati Connection*

Rose-Anne sat at her desk pondering whether to call Alex. The last time she had called and asked Alex to help her in a case, Alex had been abducted by the Chicago Mafia and almost killed. Then a crooked cop had tried to kill her, but Alex's shooting skill had saved her. She still felt guilty about having asked her.

She thought that the situation that she was going to ask for Alex's help was very different. During a recent legal seminar about the cost-free services her practice offered, she had been approached by a mother that told a her a story about a missing son. She was going to ask Alex to check into the missing person's report and see what Alex could find out.

She, after thinking it through for the third time, decided to make the call.

Alex had just ordered lunch when the harp tone phone ring let her know that her mother was on the other end. She knew that it would not be a social call at this time of day and wondered what her mother was going to throw her way.

She got up and walked out to the sidewalk so that she would not disturb the rest of the team. After their initial greeting, her mother shared her request.

Alex had one of her premonitions and she felt the hair that she knew didn't exist on the back of her neck, standing up. She knew that it seemed too simple. She asked what would happen if she found something suspicious.

Rose-Anne volunteered to call Alex's boss and see if she could convince him to assign her the case and she would arrange for the finances from her end.

Alex agreed to review the missing person's report and see what she could find out, but she reminded her mother that she needed to get permission from her boss to make it an investigative case.

When she returned to the table, Trey smiled at her, said that he recognized the ring and asked if they had just gotten a new case from Chicago.

Alex nodded and said that at the moment it was a request to check into a missing person's report but knowing her mother it most likely would turn into an assignment for the two of them.

Johnnie smiled and commented that he was glad to not be included.

Alex shook her head and said that if it became an assignment, he too would be in the middle of it. She reminded him that he had become indispensable.

Johnnie smiled and said that it was great to have such an important role on her team.

She said they should all enjoy their lunch and then walk back to the station and see what they would be doing.

The Chief was standing in the doorway to his office as they walked in. He crooked his finger and pointed into his office.

Alex, followed by Trey, walked in, and sat down. She commented that her mother must have called.

The Chief smiled and said that indeed she had and added that he had wrangled another fishing trip on the lake for himself. He said that her mother was going to make financial arrangements similar to the last time she had lured you to take a case for her. He said that he had made a deal with her to split the cost of getting a missing person's report investigated.

He added that she had pointed out that she was doing this gratis and there would be no personal gain and she had enrolled her friend the Illinois Lieutenant governor to get some funds to help.

The Chief asked what Alex knew about the request to look into the missing son of one of her mother's clients.

He then handed out two copies of the missing person's report.

He said that the two of them and of course Johnnie should look into the issue.

Alex smiled and said that his fishing offer was a better one than what she had received. She commented that the Lieutenant governor participated with her mother in providing legal help free of charge to those clients that her mother chose.

Alex replied that at that moment she had no clue about where the missing person's report would lead her.

Alex took a minute to review the missing person's report.

She then asked if Bill and Travis could be included in the investigation.

The Chief asked what she had in mind.

Alex replied that there were three high school individuals that appeared to be connected to the Red Bandana drug distribution gang. She said that she would plan to do an interview with the three and she wanted Bill and Travis to follow them afterwards to see where the three went.

The Chief nodded and said she could get them involved.

After saying, "great," she asked when her mother had invited him to go up and go fishing because she did not have an invite so far.

The Chief chuckled and said that he only needed to give a week's notice, but it could be anytime.

Alex stood up and said that he should give her the same weeks' notice and then walked out toward Bill's and Travis's desk.

She asked if the two of them were willing to get involved in a new case where the first thing she was going to ask of them was to follow three high school tough guys that seemed involved with the Red Bandana gang.

Trevor looked at Bill and commented, "see I told you that she was in convincing the Chief to give us the shit detail."

Bill smiled and replied, "but it's worse than you were thinking, she is asking us to get involved with one of the worst drug gangs in the nation."

She looked over to where Johnnie was sitting, looking at his computer and seemingly ignoring her.

She smiled and asked if he had already solved the case.

He looked at her and replied that he had no clue what he was supposed to do.

Alex gave him the name of the person submitting the missing person's report and the name of the missing person.

Johnnie typed the two names and hit the return button. He had previously set everything up so he would be able to get the missing person's report. He almost immediately had what Alex had asked him for.

He looked at Trey and Alex and said it was in their e-mail.

Alex took a quick look at the report and suggested that there would most likely be two paths in the investigation. One would be the potential drug related implications and the other would be where the missing person or his body was.

She said that she wanted to find the body and he and Bill could deal with the drug connection.

Trevor shook his head and commented that once again he and Bill got the hard and dangerous part and she and Trey got the safe and easy part.

Alex laughed and said that working with her was never easy or fair because she cherished her safety and kept her risk taking at a minimum by assigning the dangerous part to him and Bill.

Trevor smiled, nodded, and asked how many bullet holes she had in her body.

Alex nodded and replied, "too many."

Bill then added that had it not been for their Kevlar outfits all of them would have had too many as well and she would have had double the bullet hole scars that she now carried.

Johnnie commented that he had followed up on the three young men that had been named in the missing person's report and had discovered the fact that they seemed to be drug distributors for a local gang called the Red Bandanas.

Alex looked over at Trevor and asked if that gang was too dangerous for him and Bill.

Bill spoke up and said that it was becoming one of the strongest and most active gangs in the Cincinnati area and had branches in many cities across the US.

Alex then said that they, as a team, should spend some time laying out a plan on how they could all work closely together so they could watch each other's backs. She added that so far, they had been lucky to survive their interactions with the drug dealing business.

Trevor added that the Red Bandanas were known for their drive by shootings so they should all wear the Kevlar vests as a normal part of their daily attire.

Trey added that when they were on foot out on the street, they should also be alert to anyone approaching them that could draw a gun and fire. He wanted to make sure that one of them would fire first.

Alex explained about the drug connection, three high school senior bullies and the potential involvement of the Red Bandana gang and the missing person. She said that she had little hope for the missing person, but she wanted to address both sides of the issue and take out the gang as part of the case.

The Chief had joined them in the conversation and now he shook his head and said that he figured accepting a bribe to go fishing on the lake by her mother was going to cost him. He had not expected it to lead to a confrontation with some drug gang in Cincinnati.

Alex gave a laugh and said that lately fishing on the lake had been a surprise for her and that she had experienced as much gun battle action as fishing action.

The Chief's returned to his office and the team went to their favorite huddle room.

Johnnie connected his computer to the big screen and brought up the pictures of the three high school seniors. Their size and expressions seemed to fit their reputation as bullies. They were tough looking, and they each sported tattoos on their fore arms.

Alex picked out the one that was probably the ringleader and bet Trevor a cookie she was right.

Bill shook his head and said that he figured the smallest one of the three was the ringleader and he said he would put up a lunch for a tray of her cookies.

Alex liked the interaction they were having. She agreed to Bill's wager.

She then said that she wanted to arrange interviews with the three at the school. She asked Bill and Travis to wait outside of the school and be ready to tail the three and learn who in the Red Bandana gang they associated with.

Trey, who usually was the quiet one in the group, smiled and asked why Alex was picking the job that got them exposed while Bill and Travis got an easy job that let them remain in the shadows.

His comment caught Alex by surprise, and she raised one of her eyebrows and asked if he was frightened.

Trey put on a face that usually Trevor used when he complained and asked if she had read anything about the Red Bandana group and about the number of drive by shootings attributed to them.

Bill commented that Trey had given a terrible rendition of Trevor's behavior, and he should stick to his shooting and taking down gangsters.

Alex asked Bill to call the high school principal to see if they could get an interview with the three bullies.

Bill said he was going step out and make the call.

A few moments later he returned and said that he had gotten through and that the principal had agreed to arrange to have the three in his office at two.

Alex suggested they go in two cars. She said that she and Trey would go in, but Bill and Travis should stay in their car and then follow the three bullies when they got out of school.

The principal was at his desk when Alex and Trey were led in by his support. He stood up and commented that the person that had made the meeting arrangements had not let him know that the most famous Cincinnati detective was the person who was coming. He then shook hands and said that it was a privilege to be working with her. He said that he hoped she would also take the three bullies out of his school.

He then added that the three would be in his office in fifteen minutes.

He asked what the three had done to get her to come out to talk to them.

Alex replied that she was not sure. They were names in a missing person's report that was submitted for Jesse Maliber.

The principal nodded and said that he had been interviewed by a couple of officers about Jesse. He said that he had been surprised because Jesse was a good student and stayed out of trouble, did well in school and had just made the basketball team when he went missing.

Alex asked what he knew about Jesse's interaction with the three students named in the missing person's report.

The principal shook his head and said that Jesse was known to stand up to the three and had intervened multiple times in their bullying of other students.

Alex asked if he thought the three were capable of doing more than bullying.

The principal shook his head and said he had no idea, but it would not surprise him if they were.

The principal's support interrupted and let them know that the three students were in the office meeting room.

Alex followed the principal into the meeting room.

He introduced she and Trey to the three and then asked each of them to give their name.

Alex sat down across the table from the three and asked them how the day was going.

She noted that the smallest of the three was first to respond. He was the one that Bill had selected as the leader. She mentally smiled as she figured that Bill had just won a tray of her cookies.

The first to respond gave his name, Rick, and said the day was going well until they were called to the office. He pointed to the person next to him and said that he was Eli and that next to him was Sylvester.

Alex responded that the reason she had wanted to talk with them was to see if they had any idea where Jesse Maliber might be.

Rick said that they had been asked that question only a couple of months ago and their answers had not changed. They had no clue where that prick had gone but as far as he was concerned it was good riddance because the ass was always poking his nose into business that he should have stayed out of.

Alex asked what kind of business Jesse had poked his nose into.

Rick replied that Jesse was a pain in the ass and would not leave the three of them alone. He added that Jesse was a relentless bully.

Alex asked if Jesse got in the way of the three of them pushing drugs at school.

Rick put his hands on the table and looked at Alex and commented that he had been trying to be polite to a Black bitch, but he was now ending that and letting her know to mind her own business or trouble would come her way.

Alex smiled and commented that she was minding her own business and he had just stepped into her cross hairs and trouble would most likely come his way.

Rick smiled and said that he would see her outside of the school and then she would find out what it meant to get him mad.

Alex nodded and asked if that is what had happened to Jesse.

Rick looked back at her and said that he was done talking and stood up. When he stood the other two stood up and they walked out together.

Alex thanked them for their help as they walked out.

The principal said he could get security to bring them back.

Alex shook her head and said that she was quite satisfied with what she had found out.

She asked if the principal could tell where the three were going.

He made the call and let her know that the three were headed for the school's front entrance.

Alex made a quick call to alert Bill that the three were coming his way.

4 The Steep Hill

Lisa was finding it hard to concentrate on the operation. She needed to stay focused and not miss any requests the surgeon made. She had been lucky to wrangle this position. Her years of experience and the help of her friend had taken her over the job interview finish line, and she had landed this job. Finally, the operation was over, and the last suture was complete. She walked out of the surgery room and changed out of her operating room clothes. She said good night and walked to the central park that was surrounded by the two wings of the huge hospital.

She and April lived in a two-bedroom apartment located just three blocks away.

She sat down on one of the park benches and leaned back, closed her eyes, and went over all the things that had happened in the last few months.

She had listened to her son enthusiastically announce that he had made the basketball team and that he was going to buy himself a pair of Nikes with the money he had saved.

She knew that being on the basketball team was Jesse's one goal about which he was always talking.

He had spent every moment staying late at school shooting hoops and running the back and forth across the court drills. He had worked hard and had been noticed by one of the coaches.

She wiped tears from her cheeks. She was sure that the three bullies at school had something to do with Jesse's disappearance. She felt sure she had lost her son, but she wished with all her being that he might still be alive. She had so little hope of that, and more tears ran down her face. She felt a hollow in her chest that seemed larger than the Grand Canyon.

She had left Cincinnati to save her daughter who had just started at that same high school.

She knew that she had made a mistake in following the three bullies to a bar near where the police station was located. The mistake was to go into the bar and confronting the drug dealer.

That confrontation had been the catalyst for the move. It had been a hard move. She had sold or abandoned all but her personal things and come to Chicago and spent a week with an old friend who she had gone to nursing school with.

Her friend had gotten her an interview at the hospital. She knew she needed to get a job as soon as possible and felt great when she got the offer before she left the interview. Being a surgical assistance was not her first choice of what she wanted to do but it paid well, and it was the job that was offered. She took it.

She was even more lucky about finding the apartment she was now in. The hospital administrator that had interviewed her was the one that let her know about the apartment. So, on the same day she got the job, she called the realtor handling the apartment and got the apartment. She felt like she had scored two home runs on the same day. It was a great feeling that lifted her spirit.

She stood up and walked in the direction of her apartment.

Her thoughts went to the seminar that she had attended with her friend on Saturday. Because the topic was about being a woman of power and choosing to make your career one you loved, she had also convinced April to come with them.

The speaker was a lawyer named Rose-Anne Evercrest.

Refreshments were served outside of the room where the presentation was to be given. She was impressed by the fact that six round tables, each with a shrimp cocktail bowl surrounded by a variety of fruits and vegetables, was part of a free seminar.

April commented that she was glad she had come as she stood eating shrimp.

Rose-Anne came to the door of the large presentation room and invited everyone in.

She watched as April grabbed more shrimp, put them on a napkin, and carried them in with her.

The presentation was also a surprise. It was not a dry description of the services that was offered by the law office of Evercrest and Holly.

Rose-Anne welcomed everyone and then did a quick walk around the room and highlighted the services that were offered.

She then went to the speaker's podium, and asked, "Are you doing what you love to do?" The next line and then the story that followed led to the fact that a person had to follow the call of the road. She made the point that a person might begin their travel in life with the thought of doing a specific thing and then realize that what they had envisioned was not what real life delivered. It was then that one had to have the strength to choose to follow the call of the road. She then highlighted her daughter as an example. Her daughter had followed her into the practice of law and had graduated at the top of her class from Northwestern University. She had gone on to become a licensed lawyer only to discover that it was not a job that suited her. She had then looked around and chose to become a deputy in a small town just north of Chicago.

She listened as Rose-Anne admitted that at that moment she had been disappointed by her daughter, and she described how when she had asked her daughter how she could give up the great job she had, she had learned that she had a daughter that was stronger than anyone she knew.

Her daughter had replied that she wanted a more hands on life than sitting in an office being bored. She intended to seek out the bad guys and bring them to the prosecutors and a jury of their peers to make sure the bad guys ended up in jail.

She planned to be a huntress and she planned to make it a life that would constantly challenge her.

It was a great story, and it was not until the end that it hit Lisa that the person that Rose-Anne was talking about was the Cincinnati detective that she had seen several times in the news. She was the detective known as "Cincinnati's Black Annie Oakeley."

At the end Rose-Anne invited anyone that had a problem with which they were struggling with to share it with her.

She said she would be available at the refreshment tables.

When Lisa walked out, she was again surprised because the offerings on the table now were comprised of a variety of cake, rolls, punch, and other drinks.

April commented that they were greeted with hors d'oeuvres and now they got desert.

She patiently waited as various people in the audience thanked Rose-Anne for the inspirational speech. She almost gave up hope of getting to talk to her. Finally, she saw an opening, approached Rose-Anne, and shared the fact that her son had gone missing, and she wondered how she might get help in finding him.

Rose-Anne nodded and suggested they go back into the presentation room so she could get the details and see how she could help.

Lisa shared her situation and the fact that she had hurriedly moved out of Cincinnati.

Lisa was surprised when Rose-Anne said that she would get her daughter to look into her situation.

That had been on Saturday and now it was Monday, and she was wondering if anything might be happening.

She went home to her apartment with some hope in her heart and that was more than she had been expecting. She wanted to get a snack ready for when April came home. She had saved her daughter and now she had initiated some action in the search of what had happened to her son.

She did not know what else as a mother she should be doing.

Back in Cincinnati, Alex walked out of the High School thinking about what she should do next. She decided that the next day she would look into the police side of the missing person's process. She would talk to the person who handled the paperwork.

Once back in the office she planned to get Johnnie to find out who had been on the street patrolling the area around where Jesse lived. They might have seen something that was not in the missing person's report.

Bill and Trevor had easily spotted the three high schoolers as they exited the school. They followed the three. They were not surprised when about a block from the school all three of them put on red bandanas. A few moments later a black chevy passed their parked car and then pulled over and picked the three up.

Bill followed them to a small pub just a few blocks away from the police station. The black chevy parked and the three followed the driver into the bar.

Trevor commented that the drug business was right in the station's backyard. They seemed to be operating in plain sight. He wondered who on the force was getting the money to be looking the other way.

Bill said that it was time they found out. He called Alex and let her know about the situation.

Alex listened as Bill shared where he had followed the three. She was not surprised and agreed that someone on the force was looking the other way, but she said that first they were going to focus on their prime objective to find out what happened to Jesse.

Bill said he agreed and said that the three were coming back out, each carrying a backpack and were getting into the car. He would let her know where they ended up.

Alex looked at Trey who had been listening to the exchange with Bill and asked him what he thought of the situation.

Trey replied that it did not look good for Jesse if he somehow crossed wires with the Red Bandana gang. He figured the three had just gotten their next consignment of drugs that they would distribute at their high school and the surrounding area.

Alex agreed and said that at a minimum she intended to bust the three as pushers and she said they should plan to raid the location where they had picked up the drugs and see who they nabbed.

Trey suggested they call it a day and get an early start in the morning.

Alex agreed and said that the next day she wanted to talk to the person who had processed the missing person's report. She also wanted to find out which officers were out on patrol in the area around the high school on the day that Jesse went missing.

She walked in and found Johnnie at his computer.

He smiled and commented that if Matt were on shift, he would fix a quick dinner before she spent several hours on the treadmill.

Alex suggested they call ahead and order takeout at their favorite Mexican restaurant. They could ride back to the apartment where she could get ready for the gym while they waited for the food to be delivered.

She smiled and said that he might even have time to get online and solve the case.

Johnnie nodded and said that he could go along with that and if she told him where to hunt, he might have a clue how he could solve the case.

They rode back to the apartment. Alex took her bike up to the apartment and changed into her gym clothes.

A short time later Alex was at Johnnie's apartment door. She had spent the bike ride back to the apartment and the short time it took her to put her bike on her porch and to get her running shoes on thinking about the case.

More than ever, the interview of the bullies gave her the feeling that this was going to be a case that had a happy ending. She certainly could use a case that once again held a miracle.

She would ask Johnnie to look into the reports from any police units around the high school area about some sort of disturbance. If they got a break, she would have Johnnie search the system to see if he could find where Jesse was now located.

<u>5 The Red Bandanas</u>

Johnnie was at his desk doing more research about the Red Bandana gang. He found out that they were loosely associated with the Bloods crime group that had originated in California in opposition to another gang called the Crips. He determined that the gang in Cincinnati was more interested in distributing their crack cocaine and other drugs then gaining control of the entire city and county.

It seemed the local gang was not as ruthless as the West Coast Bloods. They focused more on setting up profitable networks that distributed the cocaine and other drugs to mostly high school and college customers. They did have competition and periodically gun battles emerged but quickly faded.

He learned the names of several local Red Bandana leaders and found out that they were so successful that they drove luxury cars and that the primary leader lived in an opulent multi-acre fenced in estate on the east side of town.

He located this person's offshore bank accounts that had millions of dollars in them. He was always surprised that these folks thought that their success at accumulating wealth would go on indefinitely and they stayed put instead of leaving the US, stopping their criminal activity, and then setting themselves up and living comfortable, enjoyable lives in another country.

He looked over to the huddle room where Alex and Trey were talking to the officer who had handled Lisa Maliber's missing person report. The three had entered the room some thirty minutes ago and he wondered what if anything more they had been able to learn. He knew that Alex always seemed to find some angle that led to a new investigation path. He was always amazed that her mind worked in such a nonlinear way.

He took the last sip of his now cold coffee and watched as all three walked out of the room.

He recognized the look she had on her face as she approached his desk. He was about to get asked to search out some new information.

Alex had listened carefully to the person who had handled the missing person's report. She had asked if the person had any idea which unit might have been on patrol around the area that she thought Jesse would have been in that Saturday morning.

She now had three things that she wanted Johnnie to do some research on.

First what police units might have been around the area and what they had seen.

Second, identify the most likely highways that left Cincinnati going east that a person on foot might chose to take.

And then try to determine where on the east coast Jesse might have gone.

Johnnie smiled and thanked her for only giving him three needles in a haystack. He said he would identify the police units in the next few minutes. The other two needles would take much more time.

As expected, he was able to identify the two police units that were patrolling around the area where Jesse might have been.

Alex took the information and arranged to meet the two units for lunch. At lunch, after a brief introduction she, Trey and the four officers went into the Tex-Mex restaurant and after ordering she asked if there had been anything unusual that they might have experienced on the date of the disappearance.

There was complete silence at the table. Alex was about to ask another question when one of the officers pulled out a small notebook and flipped through the pages. He held it up and pointed to the date she had given.

He commented that he had forgotten about it, but they had broken up a fight that had been going on. The person that had been getting the beating was black and had run away and the three young white men claimed that they had been attacked. The three wore red bandanas and had been the ones doing the beating. He had written their names down but when he checked there were no outstanding warrants on them.

Alex looked at the names and recognized that the three were the ones she had interviewed. They had lied to her but now she knew that they had not killed Jesse. The knowledge lifted her up like a hot air balloon leaving the ground or an Eagle rising from the surface of a lake with a fish in its claws.

The location of the beating seemed to also identify the most likely route that Jesse was likely to take.

Alex decided that she would drive the most likely route and see if she could help Johnnie find one of the needles in the haystack. She felt that in the next few days she would know where Jesse was.

As they left the restaurant, she asked Trey if he was up to a drive through the Ohio countryside.

Trey gave a laugh and said that he was sure he had no choice and suggested they stop and get a couple of drinks and some snacks to take along.

Alex agreed and suggested they get a smoothy and some pretzels.

She then took the small highway she thought was the most promising.

As they came up over a hill, Trey pointed out the small town ahead and commented that it looked like a quaint old town that was still in the pervious century.

Alex agreed. She slowed down to a crawl as they entered. She stopped in front of the only hardware/grocery store. She looked around the square and after a moment she got out and led the way into the store.

An elderly lady who was sitting on a high stool greeted her and asked how she could be of help.

Alex identified herself and Trey and asked if a few weeks ago a young Black man might have come in.

The woman nodded, gave her name as Maurine, and said that indeed a young Black man had come in. He had been polite and had been very hungry. She hoped that she had not helped a fugitive get away because she had treated him to a breakfast of a large helping of Mac and Cheese and a cup of coffee.

Alex smiled and said that no he was not a fugitive but a young man most likely trying to protect his sister and mother by disappearing. She was now trying to find him so she could link him back up with his family.

She then asked if by chance he had mentioned where he was going.

The Maurine replied that he had not but that she had told him where he might catch a bus. She added that there was a bus station in the next town east along the highway.

Alex thanked her for the information and then asked what kind of treats that she and her partner might buy.

Maurine led them back past the hardware to where there was a row candy and chips.

As they walked out to the car, Trey asked why she had bought so many bags of Godiva chocolates.

Alex replied that she had wanted to reward Maurine for the information, and she was getting ready for when they got to the bus station.

The drive to the next town took another half hour. Alex figured that it would have taken most of the day to walk that far. She estimated that Jessi would not have gotten there until late in the evening.

She led the way into the small corner bus station that was across the street from a small well-manicured maple and oak tree lined central park that had an old-fashioned Gazebo surrounded by rose plants in the center. She noted that a few red roses seem to be trying to hold on before the first of the coming frosts. She decided that this was the town that was always shown when the media wanted to show "a true American town."

Trey commented that the bushes that made a border around the park would have been a good place to spend the night.

She approached the young lady that stood behind a chest high counter at the far end of the room. She introduced both herself and Trey and the reason they were there.

The young lady introduced herself as Judy said that she could look back at the registered ticket sales if she knew the date and time.

Alex said that she could give her the one or two days, but she could not give the time for certain but that it would most likely be the evening of the first day or the morning of the second day.

Judy spent a few moments at the computer keyboard and then said that she thought she remembered selling a ticket for a bus heading for Norfolk, Virginia with a destination of Virginia Beach to a young Black man. She said that the computer let her know that he paid cash. She had put a note in that he had a backpack but no luggage. She added that she was required to put in that information. She then asked if the person was a fugitive or had committed some crime.

Alex replied that it was neither. She thanked her and asked for the best place to get a good meal.

Judy smiled and said that she recommended her aunt's diner that was just across the street and that she had recommended the same place to the person that she was looking for.

Alex handed her a small bag of the cholates and thanked her for the information and then led the way out.

Trey commented that it seemed that they were closing in on their missing person.

Alex smiled and said that she was getting a good feeling about the case and that she might have to walk along Virginia Beach as part of the search.

When they entered the diner, they were greeted by an older version of Judy, who introduced herself as Ruth and let them know that Judy had called her to let her know and had also told her about the young Black man that had eaten there a few months ago.

Alex looked at Trey and commented that news traveled fast.

Ruth gave a small laugh and said that any stranger coming into town was news that spread like a tidal wave. She said that strangers did not stay strangers long but became the focus of the local population.

She waved her hand across the nearly empty dining room and said that she would see if she had an available table or booth.

Alex said she preferred a table and pointed to one that was about in the middle.

She asked what Ruth would recommend.

Ruth replied that she had just finished a brisket pot roast that she had just put under the heat lamps, and she had steak that she had seasoned and was ready for the grill or there was a fresh garden salad waiting to be mixed. She handed Alex and Trey menus and said that she could prepare anything that was on her limited menu.

Alex said that she would go for the brisket and a small mixed salad and an iced tea.

Trey asked what cut of steak was ready for grilling.

Ruth said that it was prime T-bone and said that it came with grilled onions and blue cheese over it and the plate would have mashed potatoes and some grilled asparagus.

Alex said that he should go for the steak, and they could share.

Ruth took the order and said that she would be right out with the two iced teas and some extra plates. She commented that she liked it when her customers shared the food at the table.

She returned with the tea, four hot roll with butter at the side and the plates.

Alex asked if there was a chance that she could ask about the young Black man that had come in a couple of months back.

Ruth said that she would get her cook going and be right back.

Alex asked Trey how he thought they were doing.

Trey responded that he was getting worried that it was all going too smoothly, and he wondered when the gallows trap door was going to open.

Just as he finished, Alex's phone went off. She recognized Johnnie's ring tone called "waterfalls."

She answered and listened as Johnnie updated her on his continued data-based searches for Jesse. He thought he had found him in DC.

Alex gave a small a laugh and said he was too far north and that he should try searching for Jesse in the Virginia Beach area.

Johnnie asked how she managed to out-search his computer.

Alex replied that it was just good old fashioned foot leather detective work.

She asked how Bill and Trevor were doing.

Johnnie said he had not talked to them since she had left.

After the call ended, she put in a quick call in to Trevor.

She learned that that he had taken numerous pictures of the three bullies selling packets of drugs.

Trevor asked whether they should arrest the three and take them in.

Alex looked over to Trey who had been listening. He mouthed arrest.

Alex nodded and told Trevor to take the three in, book them and put them in holding cells. That if the three started to look like liabilities to the drug pusher, getting them off the street would most likely save their lives.

As she ended the call the cook brought out both plates. Trey had the best-looking plate that was crowned by three large onion rings. Alex's plate had the same three large onion rings garnished with cilantro.

Ruth sat down and asked how she might be of help in finding the young man.

Alex asked what Ruth may have learned while she had served him.

Ruth commented that he had ordered the least expensive item on the menu and had chosen to drink water. She knew then that he was running from something, but he was polite and even left her a nice tip. She said that he paid cash.

She said that she had asked what he was going to do when he got to where he was going, and he had said that he would need to get a job as soon as possible.

She said that was all she knew and suggested the two of them eat while the food was still hot.

Alex cut a piece of her pot roast and put it on the clean plate and pushed over to Trey.

Trey did the same with his steak.

The two of them commented how good the food was and dug in and they were both quiet for the rest of the meal.

Alex took the last sip of her iced tea. She asked Trey whether he wanted the rhubarb-cherry pie with ice cream for dessert.

Trey said he would split the desert with her.

Alex put in the order and after dessert when she paid for the dinner, she gave Ruth a bag of chocolates.

As they walked out to the car she asked if he would drive back to the station while she thought through the next steps.

Trey nodded and said that he would enjoy the drive back and asked what she had in mind.

Alex smiled and said she was thinking about going fishing.

6 Bullied Bullies

*A*lex was idly taking in the countryside as Trey drove back to Cincinnati. She looked at the time and realized that she and Trey would be back to the station well after work hours. She asked if she should call Lesley and let her know that they were still on the road back. When she got Trey's yes nod, she dialed Lesley and let her know about the road trip across much of the southern part of Ohio and that Trey was going to be late getting home. Lesley thanked her for the call and said that she would keep dinner warm.

Alex then decided to call her mother to see if she could schedule an interview with Lisa Maliber in the next day or two.

Her mother said that she could arrange for an interview after Lisa got off her shift at the hospital. She added that she thought the shift ended around four.

Alex asked Trey if a trip up on a Thursday, with an invitation for him and family to spend the weekend at her house sounded doable.

Trey smiled and commented that Nolan would be super excited, and he personally would love to go fishing as long as she kept the gun battles to a minimum.

Alex let her mother know about the weekend and listened as her mother said that it was great to have her and Trey's family for the weekend. She asked if Matt would be coming.

Alex replied that she was not sure about Matt and would call later to let her know.

Alex, after getting off the phone, asked Trey how he felt the day had gone.

Trey said that for once it seemed their case was on the good side because it seemed that Jesse was alive. He smiled and said that he was sure that Johnnie would find the exact address in the next few days.

Alex agreed and said that they should wait to celebrate because they were not done with the drug side of the case yet.

She said that she was very interested in what Jesse's mother might know. Separately she wanted to question the three drug pushing bullies that Bill and Trevor had arrested. She added that she was not really interested in them other than to get them off the street, but she was more interested in who they were pushing drugs for and in stopping that operation.

Trey nodded and said that their personal history with drug pushers gave him goose bumps. He said that they both had suffered from both beatings and shootings. He hoped that this time around they would get the upper hand from the start.

Alex smiled and asked whether he regretted being her partner.

He laughed and asked if she was kidding. Then added that she had changed his life for the better and certainly didn't blame her for what the drug kingpins had done.

Alex smiled and said he was the best partner she had ever had.

He chuckled and replied that so far as he knew he was the only partner that she had ever had.

"You're the only one but you are the best," Alex replied.

She then decided to call Matt to see what his weekend schedule would be.

Matt laughed when she asked if he wanted to go fishing and asked if they would also go apple picking for additional excitement.

Alex shook her head and said that she was beginning to think that everyone was getting the impression that she was a magnet for trouble.

Matt joked back and said that he could remind her of the gun battle on the way to the apple orchard, or the one when they had been out on the lake fishing and she had burned up a tugboat and coal barge, or the one she had when they went on vacation in Hawaii, or the one in Toronto, but he said that he wouldn't. He then said that he would trade workdays so that he could go fishing with her.

Alex thanked him for not reminding her about being a magnet for trouble.

When Alex got off the phone, Trey commented that he figured the trip to Chicago was going to be a small bit of business and a lot of family fun.

He dropped Alex off at her apartment and asked what time they would be flying out for Chicago.

Alex let him know that she had reservations for a flight at noon and that they should plan on being in the office at the regular time. She added that she planned to question the three bullies before they left for Chicago.

The next morning Trevor and Bill were sitting at their desks as Alex walked in with Johnnie. Trevor smiled and asked what had taken her so long to get to work.

Bill just shook his head and said good morning.

Alex smiled and replied that she wanted to make sure that her Bear Claw was there when she got to her desk with her coffee.

Bill handed her a Bear Claw as she got to her desk.

Alex was just putting half of it on Trey's desk as he walked in.

Trey said good morning, took a bite of the Bear Claw, a sip of his coffee and asked how they were going to handle the questioning of the three bullies.

Alex smiled and said that she thought that Bill should take the role of the good cop and Trevor should try the role of the mean cop.

Trevor flexed his arms and let out a growl. He smiled and said he was ready to be his true self and they should head for the questioning room. He suggested that they question the biggest of the three first and their small leader last. He would weave in his meanness and get them to spill all they knew.

Alex nodded and said let's do it.

Johnnie interrupted and said that he had information about the Red Bandana's boss that might make the questioning easier. He shared that it seemed that this boss had come from California where he was suspected of two murders but was not charged because no bodies had been found. He added that street rumor was that the bodies, if they were ever found, would be decomposing in lye filled drum barrels.

Alex asked Trevor if he could use this information during the questioning.

Trevor said he would have the three bullies crying before the questioning session ended.

He asked Johnnie if he could get a picture of a body in a barrel of lye. He said he recalled one being found in Mexico. He said that a picture whether it was one of the bodies in California or Mexico would make a shocking impression on the three high schoolers.

Trevor said they should go to it and get it done so that Alex could go fishing.

Alex thanked him for his support for her getting to Evenston and out on the lake.

She, Trey, and Johnnie entered the viewing room and sat down.

A moment later Johnnie announced that he had found the barrel with the body in it and said that it had a human hand floating on top, but the rest was just a murky white mess.

Bill and Trevor looked at the picture and commented that it was just what they needed.

Bill said that the two of them were ready and they should send in the first bully, and they would see how brave he was.

Alex watched as one after the other the three bullies succumbed to Bill and Trevor. She smiled and quietly said that Trevor had hit the nail on the head in suggesting the use of the visual of the barrel with the human hand floating on top. The picture broke the resistance of the bullies. They gave up the name of the person who they got the drugs from and where they were taken to pick up the drugs. They had little else to share.

They admitted to beating Jesse up, but that Jesse had run away, and they had never seen him again. They all verified that a few days later Jesse's sister had quit coming to school.

Bill let each of the bullies know that if they pushed drugs in the school or on the street he would go to the press and let the press know that the three of them had co-operated and fingered their drug contact as the boss of the Cincinnati Red Bandana drug cartel.

Each of the three said that was not fair because they did not have a choice and they did not want to end up in a barrel.

Bill suggested that they plead guilty to distributing drugs and he would see that they served their sentence in a low security prison facility where they would be out of the reach of the person that was supplying the drugs.

Each separately agreed. The leader was not going to agree until Bill made the point that his two buddies had already agreed.

Bill asked for all three to be brought in together. He wanted to review the paperwork with their admission to pushing drugs at the high school and on the area around the high school.

He read the confession to the three of them at the same time and asked that each sign a copy of the admission paperwork.

After signing the three were led away and taken to holding cells.

Alex entered the questioning room and congratulated Bill and Travis for the great job they had done.

When they were all together, Johnnie laughed and commented that he had super imposed the floating hand because the barrel that had the body in it only had a very decomposed body that was not visible through the white murky haze.

Alex let Johnnie know that she would give him a tray of cookies for his creativity.

Travis asked how many cookies came with the congrats on the good job that he and Bill had done.

Alex smiled and replied that they would each get a tray of her cookies. But for a tray, she wanted to know who came to the hearing for the three bullies. She was sure that the internal leaker would get the word out to the drug boss. She wanted to see if they could figure out who the internal leak might be, and she wanted to know which lawyer might be working with the drug boss.

Bill said that they would make sure to get a picture of everyone that came to the hearing and get Johnnie to find out who they were.

Alex looked at Trey and said that it was time for them to catch a flight to Chicago where they had important work to get done.

Trevor smiled and said that he too always figured putting a worm on a hook was very important work.

Alex turned, waved over her shoulder, and commented that she loved him too.

7 Regrets

Jesse looked at the three pictures he had hung up on the wall in front of his work desk. Two were framed certificates that were on either side of the third picture of his mother with her hands over his and his sister's shoulders. One certificate was his High School Diploma that he had earned in a short two months and the other was his certificate of completion to be an IT programmer. He felt very lucky to land an IT role with a large company that let him work remotely. He was getting paid more than he had thought he would ever earn.

He still held the goal of getting a college education, but he figured that he would save up for it and perhaps do a lot of the work at a local junior college.

He had immediately set up a bank account where his paycheck was being sent.

He was just getting started and hoped that he would soon be able to move to a better place to live and maybe even get a car so he could get around.

He tried to see if he could find out how his mother and sister were doing but had no luck online. He decided to take a trip to Cincinnati to find out in person, but he did not yet want to make contact. He wanted to make sure that he did not trigger some sort of retribution by the three bullies against them.

This time he had enough money for the bus ride and to feed himself.

His trip to Cincinnati was a bust. He found out that his mother and sister had moved. He had no clue where they might have gone. He went to the hospital where his mother worked and asked for her but was informed that she no longer worked there. He tried to get her address but the only thing he learned was that she had moved away from Cincinnati.

He returned to Virginia Beach and tried to think how he might be able to find them.

Little did he know that he was going to be the one to be found.

Johnnie had been scouring the internet for some clues about where on the east coast Jesse had chosen to locate. He succeeded when he found a certificate of completion on a site that claimed to train and get jobs for people who graduated from their program for a Jesse T. Maliber of Viginia Beach. He dug a little deeper and got the address that Jesse had given in his application to the school.

He did additional follow up and found the e-mail sent to Jesse and followed up on all the job applications he had sent out. He was impressed with Jesse's thoroughness and the number of applications he had sent out.

He found the three that had offered him a job and then zeroed in on the acceptance by Jesse. He had accepted the offer that allowed him to work remotely. It was not the highest dollar offer but the feature of being able to work from anywhere in the country must have been what Johnnie figured had made the difference for Jesse.

He sent the information to Alex so that she would have it when she interviewed Jesse's mother.

The plane was just pulling up to the gate when she received Johnnie's message and the information he had collected. She shared this with Trey and asked how they should use the information when they interviewed Jesse's mother and sister.

Trey suggested that they wait until they had concluded the interview and had gathered the information that his mother and sister might have about Jesse's disappearance. He said that the decision to move to Chicago might have been based on more than Jesse's disappearance. Jesse must have left under duress and perhaps to protect his mother and sister.

Alex agreed with Trey and said that they should concentrate on getting to her house and finding out what her mother had planned for dinner. She added that she hoped not to gain too many pounds due to her mother's cooking.

During the ride to the house, where she had grown up, she decided to call Bill to see if they had any additional information.

Bill replied that he had asked Johnnie to continue to dig into the Red Bandana organization to see what else they could learn. He said he was interested in the source of the drugs that were being distributed.

He shared that some of the drugs were being produced locally. He chuckled and said that the location was a small building that had been a firehouse that was close to where the Body Parts group had set up their operation that had subsequently burned down. He commented that it was somewhat ironic that had the fire house been in operation they might have kept the fire from destroying the building housing the body parts operation.

Alex thanked him for continuing to dig into the drug side of the case. She said that the happier side of the case would most likely end on a high note, and afterwards she wanted to shut down the Red Bandana operation.

She asked Bill if he was willing to go to Virginia Beach and verify that the person that Johnnie had found was the Jesse Maliber they were looking for. If it turned out that he was the one, then he should see if he were willing to meet with his mother on a fishing trip out on Lake Michigan.

Bill agreed that he and Trevor would fly out and get a positive identification and asked whether the two of them should escort Jesse on the fishing trip.

Alex gave a laugh and said that the trip would be on her and that their spouses were invited as well.

Alex heard Trevor in the background shout out that he would put the worm on her hook, and he would also bring a case of beer.

She then called Johnnie to invite him to join the fishing trip.

Johnnie thanked her for the invitation but said that he and Mary had plans for the weekend but that she should bring him a fish that he would prepare for her and Matt.

She said goodbye as Trey turned into the driveway to her parents' house.

The trees on either side of the long driveway had continued to grow and had formed a tunnel that framed the center of the house. She noticed immediately the round flower bed at the center of the circle driveway had yellow roses in full bloom.

Rose-Anne had been waiting for Alex and Trey and rushed out when they drove into the circle.

Alex congratulated her mother on the prominent display of yellow roses blooming in the center circle garden. She said that it was the first time she had seen them and asked when they had been planted.

Rose-Anne led her over to the edge of the garden and commented that she, with some help, had planted them the day before especially for her favorite daughter.

Alex looked at Trey and commented that now she knew where she had gotten that phrase, "favorite partner."

Trey chuckled and replied, "like mother, like daughter."

Rose-Anne said she had no clue what they were talking about, but they should all go into the house and after they put their stuff into their rooms, they should all meet out by the pool for a casual dinner.

When she walked out to the pool, Alex could tell that her mother had ordered the food from her Pizzeria. The onion rings were stacked up on a vertical holder, three varieties of pizza were offered on a large platter and a variety of non-alcoholic drinks were in a large ice filled bucket.

Her father was now home and sitting at the pool side table. He got up and gave her a hug and let her know that her Jaguar was in the garage and ready for her to drive.

Alex took a nonalcoholic beer, opened it, took several onion rings, and sat down next to him.

She asked her mother how business was going at the Pizzeria.

Rose-Anne smiled and said that ex-sheriff, Jason Shephard was personally making it a success. He had introduced the onion rings, cheese sticks and a few additional sides. He listened to his customers, and it resulted in a whopping thirty percent business revenue increase.

She said that it was even better because she, Jason, and his wife all got along, and Jason's wife had taken a full-time position as front cashier and waitress.

Alex nodded and said that it made her feel good that he had found the work that let him enjoy his day. He had been a great first boss when she had decided to get into the field of police work.

Trey had come out to the pool and had listened to the discussion about the sheriff and commented that he had a chance on the last trip to talk to him and had learned about all of Alex's weaknesses from him and that it had made a huge difference in how carefully he treated her.

Alex laughed and said that she loved him too.

Rose-Anne asked Trey how the family was doing and what time they would arrive.

Trey gave her the time on Friday afternoon when they would arrive and commented that Nolan was super excited about coming up and that Lindsey said she was looking forward to taking it easy. He said that Lindsey said hello and thanked her for being so gracious.

Alex asked what boat they would be going out on.

Her father smiled and said that Dexter insisted that they take his Golden Goose and that he would personally skipper her.

Alex said that was great, but she wanted to make sure that she paid for the use of the yacht. She added that she knew that Dexter would not accept payment, but she would give the appropriate amount to his favorite charity.

Her father nodded and said that Dexter had commented about payment and that she would have free rides on the Golden Goose for as long as he ran the marina. He commented that he still felt guilty for aiding his college friend's attack on her.

Alex shook her head and commented that his friend had almost sunk the Golden Goose and that he was not responsible for his friend's actions. He certainly did not "aid" him.

And to boot, the fishing boat that his friend had used was a total loss.

Her father said that made logical sense, but it was not how Dexter took it.

Alex asked Trey if he was OK with her picking Harold Zimmerman's Aunt's restaurant as the location for the lunch the next day. He responded that the location did not matter to him and figured she would pick a good place.

Alex called the restaurant and made reservations for the private room. The receptionist said that the room was usually reserved for larger groups and asked if a booth or table would be acceptable.

Alex replied that she needed the room so she could do a very personal interview. She referenced Harold as a person that could be contacted if there were any additional questions. She made the point that she would pay whatever the price was for the room.

Once the reservation was made, she focused back on the dinner and the conversation at the table.

The evening went well into the night. Alex was in no hurry to go to bed. She figured she would sleep in at least until eight in the morning. The lunch interview on the following day was the only work item.

She wanted to enjoy driving her Jag but she figured that they should take the SUV so they could both host Lisa and her daughter and take them to lunch and then afterwards go to the airport and pick up Lesley and Nolan.

Trey had come down early the next morning and was enjoying a cup of coffee and talking to Rose-Anne. He had enjoyed breakfast with Russel who left right after so he could get ready for an early morning lecture.

Alex came down the back stairs that entered directly into the kitchen and smiled when she saw her mother and Trey chatting. She knew that her mother was fond of Trey and had a very positive impression of his character.

Her mother asked what she wanted for breakfast.

Alex replied that a soft-boiled egg, a piece of buttered toast and jam and a cup of coffee would be all she wanted.

She asked when her mother needed to get to work.

Rose-Anne smiled and said that she was working from home and that she worked from home almost every Friday and that often she would do a little work on Saturday as well as Sunday. It allowed her to manage her time in a flexible manner. She added that she had made the workday change for all the people in the office.

Alex said that it seemed to be a good way to keep from having Friday be a stressful day.

Rose-Anne asked if she was planning to use the Jag. She added that her father had taken it in and had it serviced, tuned up and had it detailed. She added that he periodically drove it to keep it in shape.

Alex replied that though she would love to drive the Jag, using the rental for the day would provide the room they needed. They would first ferry Lisa and her daughter and go to lunch. Then after that they could go to the Airport and pick up Lesley and Nolan and have plenty of room for the luggage.

Rose-Anne said that the dinner was coming mostly from the Pizzeria, but it would not be pizza. Sylvester was preparing T-bone steaks for everyone, and the sides would be cold slaw, baked potato, and onion rings. Her contribution was to make a cucumber and tomato salad. She asked if that would be enough or should she add something more.

Alex commented that she would eat a light lunch so that she would have room for what sounded like a huge dinner. She asked if Sylvester would eat dinner with them.

Rose-Anne said that he planned to only cater the dinner, but she added that he and his wife would be part of the group going fishing.

Alex nodded and said that she looked forward to chatting with him when they went fishing.

Later, on the drive to downtown Chicago, Trey asked how Alex was going to handle the interview.

Alex replied that she would ask leading questions and then listen carefully to the replies. She said she agreed with him that the move away from Cincinnati might have been triggered by more than just Jesse's disappearance.

Trey nodded and commented that when the drug trade was mixed with family affairs things could be very messy.

When they arrived at the hospital where Lisa worked, they found a parking spot that let them see the front door.

Alex commented on the large size of the park that the Hospital wings surrounded. She added that on a clear day like the one they were enjoying, it felt like she was at the bottom of the pool looking up through the water.

A few moments later, Trey pointed to a person exiting the hospital and asked if it was Lissa Maliber and her daughter.

Alex said she thought so and opened the door and got out. She walked over to where the two were standing, introduced herself and Trey and then verified their identity. She complimented both on their dresses.

Lissa thanked her for the compliment and added that she was so happy that she had lucked out and met her mother and that she was the mother of the most successful detective in Cincinnati.

Alex smiled and replied that her success was due to a partner like Trey and a team of supporting detectives.

She pointed to the SUV and suggested they go to lunch.

A few minutes later they arrived at the restaurant and were escorted into the private room. Harold Zimmerman's aunt came in and apologized for the initial problem Alex had in getting the room. She said that dessert would be on her. She suggested the strawberry rhubarb pie with a scoop of vanilla.

Alex thanked her for such a kind gesture and asked what she recommended for lunch.

The recommendation was a slice of heart of shoulder roast beef with gravy, roast asparagus and mashed potatoes smothered in butter.

Alex smiled and said it sounded very good. She looked around and asked if there were any takers.

Both Lissa and April said that the recommendation sounded great and asked to have iced tea with it.

Alex said that though it sounded delicious she knew that her mother was having a special dinner catered so she was going for a small mixed salad and a lemonade.

Trey said he would have the same since he too would be at the dinner.

Lissa commented that she had learned that Alex's mother was also known to be a chef.

Alex nodded and said that she had chef friends all around the world. She added that the evening dinner would be catered by a family friend and not prepared by her mother.

Once the drinks arrived Alex asked Lissa to share with her what had happened when Jesse had failed to come home.

Lissa thought for a minute and then said that on that first day she had gone out all around the neighborhood trying to find him.

She had then called several of his friends to see if they knew where he might be. She had then tried to put in a missing person's report but was told she would have to wait for twenty-four hours.

The next day, a Saturday, she followed the three bullies that Jesse had told her about. She followed them to a bar only a few blocks away from the downtown police station. The three had gone in and when they came out their backpacks were bulging. She figured they had gotten a supply of drugs.

She admitted that she wanted to scream at them that they were horrible individuals, but she had turned so they could not see her face.

She then went into the police station and put in the missing person's report. She made sure their names were in the report.

She looked over at Alex and said that then she had done something stupid and gone back to the bar. She went in and confronted the person that she suspected was the local drug dealer.

The lunch order was being brought in and she stopped talking.

Once the food was all on the table, Alex asked Lissa to continue.

Lissa nodded and then said that going into the bar was a huge mistake. She had confronted the person who seemed to be in charge. His response was to threaten to kill her and put her in a barrel of lye.

He had smiled and said that he would make sure her daughter would join her in the barrel where they could be together for eternity.

She had almost run out of the bar and had gone home, called her friend in Chicago and asked if she could come up and stay until she got a job there. The next day she packed up the few things she owned, cancelled her apartment rental agreement, took April out of school, and drove the rental moving truck to Chicago.

She admitted that once she was on the road, she felt a huge weight lift from her shoulder.

She went on to say that things in Chicago had gone very well. She got a job almost immediately. She was able to get April into school and found an apartment that she could afford in the following week.

She focused on getting into her work and getting oriented at the hospital.

Then one day she had attended Alex's mother's conference on legal support and now she was talking to her.

Alex asked April what she knew about the three bullies.

April said they were terrible guys who were always picking on some girl or other. They seemed to get away with doing whatever they wanted.

Her brother was one of the few guys who stood up to them and refused to let them have their way. He had several fights with them in school and always came out on top because he had his own friends who would help him.

It was clear to her that the three bullies only acted when they had a person outnumbered.

The Friday afternoon that he had left to go to buy his shoes he let her know that afterwards he planned to go back to the gym at school and shoot hoops. She had not seen him since that afternoon.

Alex let them know that the three bullies were under arrest for distributing drugs and would end up serving time.

She added that she knew about the leader of the Red Bandanas who was the drug dealer in the bar. He would be arrested and charged once she got done with her investigation of the missing person's report.

She added that he was a person who had left California where he was suspected of killing several people and putting them in a fifty-gallon barrel full of lye.

She looked over to Lissa and said that her decision to leave had most likely been a wise one.

Lissa thanked her for the information. She added that at the time she had thought she was a bit fanatical.

Alex then asked if the two of them liked to fish.

Lissa replied that was one of the things she, Jesse and April had done often because it was one of the least expensive ways to spend a day along the Ohio River. She said she loved to fish.

Alex then invited the two of them to go out with her on Lake Michigan to fish.

Lissa thought for a minute and asked if this meant that there was bad news and taking her fishing was a way to soften the news.

Alex said that on the contrary and that the invitation gave her more time to pursue a much more positive approach.

After lunch Alex took Lissa and April to their apartment and after making sure they understood that a cab would be at the curb at five in the morning to take them to the marina where she would meet them, she and Trevor left for the airport.

8 Maliber Reunion

Camacho sipped on his beer and stared into the mirror across the bar from him. He took in the silver streak in his otherwise black hair. He figured it indicated how the past few years weighed heavy. The law in California had forced him to move out and now he was in sleepy, slow moving Cincinnati pushing drugs in the surrounding area. He was trying to be as low key as possible and to avoid conflict with the other drug dealers already established in the area.

The most lucrative areas were the high schools, the university and surprisingly the business district. He also covered all the poorer areas, but they were harder to manage. His high school pushers were the easiest to manage and to collect from. The business professionals needed to be discreet and made the drug transfer a delicate dance.

He shook his head as he thought about the most recent confrontation that he had had with an angry mother who had accused him of hurting her son. He had threatened to eliminate her, and she had bolted out of the bar.

He probably should have kept his threat to himself.

He had sent a couple of his men out to round her up. They came back with the news that she had left town and there was no forwarding address.

He found out from the three high schoolers pushing for him in that area that they had a run in with her son. The three were in the process of beating the hell out of him when a squad car came by and stopped the fight. The person they were beating had run away and escaped. They had not seen him since that afternoon.

He now understood the confrontation he had had with the angry mother. He had little concern about that situation. He just moved on. That family was not a threat to him or his business.

What worried him more was that the three said that they had been interviewed by a Black female detective and her partner about the missing son and about their involvement in pushing drugs. When they gave him her name a cold shiver went down his back. He knew her reputation. She had made news that had reached him when he was still on the West Coast. Now she was very close to his doorstep. So close in fact, not only because his center of operation was only a few blocks from her office, but also because she had interviewed three of his pushers. He figured he would need to eliminate the three.

He thought through his options. He might not need to do a thing, but he figured he should think through all the options.

He could relocate his operation away from Cincinnati. This, however, would most likely put him in conflict with some other drug distributors and he would have to establish a presence by force. That was always a very risky thing to do.

His other option was to put the Black detective so to say in the barrel. He figured he could skip the barrel and just have one of his guys shoot her.

He contacted his police informant to find out her address. He then scoped out the location and the place where a sniper could be located. He found the place from where he would shoot and figured that one shot would eliminate his main problem.

He returned to his normal bar office location and relaxed. He made a call to a professional sniper and arranged for the kill. He assigned one of his men to be a spotter to watch the apartment entrance and get the timing of when the sniper would need to be in place. He was set and confident that it would soon all be cleaned up and he could continue doing business as usual.

Bill and Trevor flew to Norfolk and then drove out to the address on Virginia Beach. Johnnie had provided them with the address and a picture of the apartment building, so they were confident that they were at the right place. They rang the entrance doorbell and identified themselves to the person answering the bell. They entered and took the elevator to the fifth floor.

They knocked on the apartment door and were greeted by Jesse.

Bill introduced himself and Trevor. He verified that Jesse was from Cincinnati.

Jesse asked how they had found him and was he in trouble.

Trevor chuckled and said that maybe he was in trouble with his mother but not with the law.

Bill explained that his mother had obtained the help of someone in Chicago, who had contacted the Cincinnati Detective department. He was listed as a missing person and through some detailed investigation had been located. They were there to invite him to a fishing family reunion.

Jesse said he had never heard of the police inviting someone to go fishing.

Bill smiled and replied that he would meet a detective and her family that loved to go fishing and who was inviting him to a fishing family reunion.

Trevor then handed Jesse his airplane tickets for that afternoon.

Jesse looked at the first-class tickets to Chicago. He looked at Bill and said that he had never flown first class, in fact he had never flown anywhere. He looked at the ticket again and let out a low whistle and said that he hoped they treated the passengers in first with special kid gloves.

Bill said they were all sitting in first class compliments of Alex Evercrest, the lead detective on the case.

Trevor handed Jesse his hotel reservations in Evanston, Illinois and said they were all staying at the same hotel. He asked if Jesse could be packed and ready to go in the next hour or so because the plane would not wait.

Jesse nodded and asked if they might want a coffee or something else to drink or to snack on. He commented that he felt a little disoriented by the invitation to go fishing as part of a family reunion and flying first class all seemed to be the buzz that came along with a high.

Bill said that he had been disoriented ever since he had started working with the detective, he would meet on the fishing trip.

"She is definitely a unique person," Trevor piped in.

Not long after they were on their way. The flight was only a couple of hours. The trip to the hotel took as long as the flight. They all checked into the hotel just before dinner.

Both Bill and Trevor's wives had already checked in and said they would meet them in the dining area.

Bill extended a dinner invitation to Jesse who accepted.

It was pitch black when Alex looked out her window. The big blue numbers on the clock clicked over to five. She wanted to roll over but instead she sat up.

She pushed on Matt. Leaned over and gave him a kiss on the cheek and said it was time to go fishing.

He got up and walked into the bathroom.

She got up, got ready and went down to the kitchen where she knew a cup of coffee would be waiting for her.

She was finally getting to drive her Jag to the fishing pier.

Lesley led a sleepy-eyed Nolan into the kitchen and joined in having a cup of coffee. Nolan sat down on the floor against the wall and closed his eyes.

Alex suggested that they take off for the marina and get on board the Golden Goose and then enjoy a great breakfast of pancakes drenched in maple syrup, have a side sausage patty and cup of black coffee.

She led the way to the garage. Lesley and Nolan got into the back seat and Matt sat in the front seat. The drive to the marina was one of silence.

She hoped that all the folks would make it on time.

She could see the lights on the Golden Goose as she parked her car. She led the way and boarded. She smiled when she saw that all the ingredients to make breakfast had been put out along the counter.

She asked Nolan if he was ready for some breakfast.

He nodded and laid his head on the table.

She started the breakfast preparation.

A few moments later, Alex watched as Lissa and April got out of a cab. She asked Leslie to handle the pancake and walked out onto the pier. She waved at the two and they walked toward her. A black SUV entered and parked in the parking lot. She saw Trey and the rest of her family got out.

Alex led Lissa and April onto the Golden Goose and asked what they would like for breakfast.

A few moments later Jason and his wife arrived.

Alex was pleased that everything was happening in the sequence that she had hoped.

Bill waited until six thirty as Alex had requested and then he drove to the marina. He knew that Alex was staging his arrival so that it would be a surprise to Jessi's mother.

The sun was just threatening to come over the horizon when he parked next to the black SUV.

He had Trevor lead the way with the two wives and he and Jesse followed. He had asked Trevor to have his camera ready to take pictures of the reunion.

Alex watched as Trevor led the way. She distracted Lissa and April, so they were looking at the sun that was just breaking the horizon.

Jessi was the first to speak and say hello and rush forward as Lissa stood up. The scene was one of hugging, kissing and tears.

Lissa turned to Alex and told her that she would never forget this moment, gave her a hug, and thanked her.

Dexter came on board and asked if it was time to cast off.

Alex nodded and said that they should all enjoy the ride and get ready to fish once they were at her favorite spot on the lake.

The fishing was good. She caught one that she planned to take back for Johnnie and then stopped fishing. Everyone caught at least one and then enjoyed grilled hamburgers, bratwurst, and hot dogs for lunch.

The Maliber reunion was a continuous cycle of tears, hugs, and laughter.

Alex sat with Bill, Trevor, and Trey. She commented that they should all cherish the moment when they could enjoy a happy ending to part of their case.

Trevor nodded and added that he would remember this one for quite a while. He commented that he now knew how Alex felt about finding and saving Annie and her two daughters.

Alex smiled and said that it was a feeling that she always embraced when a case was trying to pull her down.

Trey pointed over to where Matt was playing checkers with Nolan and added that seeing Nolan play with Annie's two daughters always brought back the memory of watching Alex run out ahead of him to get to Annie and her two daughters so that she could save them from a deranged kidnapper. What stood out was that she had stepped in between Annie and the deranged kidnapper and taken a bullet in the arm and in the chest even as she shot and killed him.

Trevor then said that he really loved Alex for who she was.

Alex shook her head and said that she was going to sit with Lesley, and the rest of the women.

Dexter announced that he was shutting down the grill and would soon point the Golden Goose toward the harbor.

Dinner that night was a continuation of the reunion of Jesse and his mother and sister.

Alex was enjoying catching up with her first boss. She learned that he and his wife were having the best time of their lives in running the Pizza shop and in exploring the area that they had lived all their lives but seen so little of.

He asked her how working in Cincinnati was going. He commented that he had kept up with her many cases and talked to her boss frequently.

Alex smiled and said that she thanked him for his original recommendation and that Cincinnati was a wonderful place in which to work and to play. The only issue was that she was often on cases that pulled her away to other cities and locations.

He looked over to where Matt was playing with Nolan and Trey and asked whether she had found her soul mate in Cincinnati.

Alex shook her head and said that they had met in the deep south during one of her cases. He had followed her to Cincinnati and made it clear that he was after her. She added that he was the soul mate she had been looking for.

Jesse came over and thanked her for arranging for him to meet back up with his mother and sister. He let her know that he was planning to move to Chicago as soon as his lease in Virginia ended. He planned to stay in Chicago for another week and asked if the return ticket would still be good and if he could downgrade it and use the money.

Alex nodded and said that it was his ticket, and he should do what he wanted with it.

The next morning after a light breakfast, she, Matt, Trey, Lesley, and Nathan all rode together to the Airport. The flight back to Cincinnati was uneventful.

They parted ways at the luggage area. Lesley had suggested a picnic and they had agreed to figure out where to go during the week.

She sat quietly on the drive to the apartment. The weekend had been a great success. It was the part of the case that would rate as the number two of getting loved ones together. She had a handful of young women she had saved who stayed connected with her and that as a group was the number three set of positive memories. She figured that saving Annie and her two daughters would remain number one forever.

Matt knew that this case was one that Alex was feeling positive about. He hoped that the second part of the case could be handled quickly and with the success that Alex always seemed to accomplish.

He drove his van into the parking garage that was across the street from the apartment building and parked in his reserved spot. Each apartment had an assigned spot that they paid for, but it made it easier to have a reserved spot, so he thought it was worth it.

He got his luggage out and then followed as Alex walked out and got ready to cross the street.

Suddenly he spotted a red dot on the back of her neck. He lunged forward and knocked her down and felt a burning sting in his left shoulder.

Alex was surprised at Matt's sudden push, but her impulse reaction took over and she rolled, pulled her weapon, located the barrel of a rifle pointing down from the top of the parking garage and fired.

The shooter was surprised at the fast reaction of the person behind his target. He tried to hold his shot, but it was too late. The bullet hit the guy instead of his intended target. He leaned forward to get a second shot.

He felt the bullet hit and suddenly he realized he was falling and then the world went black.

Alex jumped up and checked to make sure the shooter was dead. She kicked his weapon away and then went to Matt.

Matt lay still as he realized he had been shot. He wondered if his EMT team would be the ones that would show up.

He looked up at Alex and asked if she had killed the shooter.

He could hear the sirens and knew that in a few minutes the two of them would be surrounded by police and the EMT's.

He smiled and said that he preferred to pick apples on a warm fall morning.

Alex gave him a kiss on the forehead and said she thanked him for the push, and she was sorry that he had taken the bullet.

Matt looked up and laughed when he realized it was his team that was going to treat him. He said hello as they went into action and strapped him to the board and soon, they had him in the van and were driving off.

Alex verified where they were going and let Matt know she would bring him a treat once he was in his room.

She then held up her shield and walked over to the policeman that seemed to be in charge and identified herself. She pointed to where she had put her weapon down on the ground. She described what had happened and said that she did not know who the shooter was or why she had become his target.

She walked over to where the coroner's team had turned the body over. She asked to take a picture of his face.

It took almost a half an hour for the scene to be processed.

She made sure it was OK to leave the site of the crime and then took the suitcases to her the apartment.

Then she went down to see if Johnnie was in his apartment. When he opened the door, she entered and let him know what had just happened.

Johnnie commented that he had been in the shower and by the time he had gone out to see what had happened the coroner's van was driving away.

Alex asked if he could track the shooter down using the picture that she had taken.

Johnnie opened his computer and said he would give it a try.

He asked if Alex wanted some of her own cookies and a cup of tea or coffee. After having poured two cups of coffee he began his search.

A few minutes passed then his computer gave a drum roll and flashed three times and the on-screen picture had a name and a list of priors. He was a member of the Reds in LA and wanted for murder.

Alex then asked Johnnie to share the information with Bill, Trevor, Trey, and the Chief and let them know that on Monday she planned to arrest and bring in the local Red Bandana leader and charge him with attempted murder.

She then asked if Johnnie had any extra cookies that she could take to Matt at the hospital.

9 Robin Hood

The evening news came through to Camacho like a hundred police sirens wailing in the night. The assassin from LA that he had contracted and had just paid had been killed but his target was unscathed.

He hoped that his connection to the assassin would be untraceable. It was a verbal agreement and a ten thousand dollar up front, and it would have been another ten thousand after the kill.

He felt he was fine, but he had to admit that he was as nervous as a cat in a room full of rocking chairs. He needed to get his tail out of the room.

Not having heard from his three high school distributors who had put him on the trail of eliminating the Black detective made him even more nervous.

He did not like being in the dark and uninformed. He was used to being in control and keeping others in the dark or putting them permanently in the dark.

Johnnie waited for Alex in the hallway across from the elevator. He knew that she had stayed with Matt in the hospital until at least midnight. He hoped she was wide awake and ready to go.

She had sent out a message that she wanted to shut down the Red Bandanas. He was sure that meant some digging on his part. He just needed to know what she wanted so he could focus his effort. He knew Alex as always would want to move fast and he knew when she was attacked, she would move faster than an eagle diving for a trout in a lake.

Alex stepped out of the elevator, greeted Johnnie, and guided her bike toward the door. She was certain that the shooter who she had killed was hired by Comacho Lopez. She was trying to figure out how to prove it. She needed to get something that linked the shooter to him. She had to find some physical evidence. There might be a phone conversation and there might be traceable cash. She was going to see if Johnnie could use his hacking skills to give her the edge. The assassin had failed but he had made the situation very personal. As personal as if he had tried to sleep with her instead of just kill her. She was in a vengeful mood.

The ride to the station was silent. She was trying to think how she was going to get some sort of evidence to connect the shooter to Comacho.

She changed into her work outfit, got a cup of coffee, and walked toward her desk. She saw that Bill and Trevor were at their desks and there was a half of bear claw on her desk and the other half on Trey's desk.

She picked it up, took a bite and thanked whoever was so kind to as to get her started.

Trey walked in and said hello and asked when he was going to be able to shoot a local drug dealer.

Trevor shook his head and asked what Trey had eaten for breakfast.

Trey just shook his head and said that at this moment he wanted his sniper rifle and a target to take out.

He asked Alex how Matt was doing.

Alex said that he was feeling fine when she left him late the past night. He said that the team should nail whoever had set up an assassin to kill her.

Johnnie took a sip of his coffee and asked how he could help nail the perp to the wall.

Alex said she needed to find the link between Camacho and the shooter. They had the identity of the shooter, but they had yet to find out how he had gotten to Cincinnati. Where he was staying. How he got paid. Where he had obtained his weapon. How he had known where she lived.

Johnnie opened his computer and began typing. A few moments later he said he had the rental car information for a John Smith for a grey sedan and he had a license plate number. He asked if a car had been found that may have been driven by the assassin.

Bill dialed the dispatcher and asked which units had processed the shooting scene. A few moments later he was talking to somcone that had been at the scene. He asked if they had found a car and gave him the license plate number.

He got off the phone and said that a unit was going to drive through the parking garage and all the close-by parking lots to see if they could find the car. They would call if they found the car.

Alex asked if Johnnie had the time when the shooter had landed in Cincinnati.

Johnnie worked for a few more minutes and said that he thought it would have been a red eye special from LA that had landed at five thirty Sunday morning. The car rental was at seven.

Alex nodded and asked if there was any way he could get into the computer system of the bar that Camacho used as his headquarters.

Johnnie said that maybe he could walk past the bar and find out if there was a local area network inside. If there was, he could get the name and then he would be able to hack in.

He said that he would go home and get into his bum's uniform and then take a walk past the bar. If he got the hubs name, he would cross the street and put out his hat and hack in.

Bill said that he and Trevor would follow about a block behind him and then turn around when he crossed the street, and they would walk back toward the police station.

Johnnie nodded and a said that once he was in, he would see if he could link into the bar's hub or hubs to the cloud so he could access them remotely.

Alex then asked what had happened to the weapon that the shooter had used. She made a call and found out it was in the evidence holding area. It had been processed and the fingerprints entered into the database.

Alex asked if the rifle's owner could be identified.

She was told that there were no noticeable serial numbers. She asked for the weapon to be sent to the lab to see if they could get a serial number from it.

Johnnie ran the fingerprints that had been on the weapon and came up with the actual name of the shooter. He was a freelance assassin that worked for anyone willing to pay his fees and expenses. He was formally linked to the Reds gang in LA.

The call came in that the car had been found in a parking lot two blocks from the location where the shooting had taken place.

Alex asked that the car be isolated, and she would be over immediately to field process it. She led the way out to her car and she and Trey went to the parking lot where the rental was located. She asked one of the policemen to unlock the car.

The front and back seats were empty. She popped the trunk and found what she had been looking for.

She unzipped a black sports bag and found it full of money. There was a carrying case for a rifle and extra ammunition. She bagged the sports bag in a large evidence bag and then told the officers to have the car towed to the evidence parking area and have it processed. She told them that it should not be torn up but only processed for fingerprints.

She then drove back to the station and took the evidence bags into the main work area.

Johnnie knew immediately what the sports bag held and what Alex was going to ask him to do. He walked toward their favorite huddle room and set up his computer.

Alex put the rifle holder on her desk and asked Bill to have it processed for fingerprints.

She carried the sports bag with the money to the huddle room. She opened the bag and counted the bundles of banded bills as she laid them out on the table. There were fifty bundles. She counted one bundle and found out that each bundle was two thousand dollars and made up of one-hundred-dollar bills.

She asked Johnnie if he would be able to trace the bills.

Johnnie said that they looked new and fresh and that he should be able to find the bank that had last processed the bills. He took one number and began to check which bank might have issued it.

A few moments later he said he had the bank. He then spent the next few moments poking around the bank's database and found a series of bill numbers that were withdrawn at the same time and the number on the one bill he had started with.

Alex and Trey had been entering the numbers of bills into their shared database so that Johnnie could process them.

He commented that there had to be another bank because the amount withdrawn from the one, he was in was not enough to cover the number of bills on the table.

Johnnie verified that all the bills in the bundle where his first bill had come from were withdrawn at one time.

He then began to run the rest of the numbers. He found three additional local banks.

He also found out that the withdrawal happened on different days of the week and always at some level that would not draw attention because the amount was always below five thousand.

Alex asked if he could hack into the bar's computer and see if there was any accounting information that might link the money withdrawn or any other transaction with the banks. She commented that if there was money to withdraw then there must be money deposited.

She figured that there might also be links to other banks.

She let Johnnie know that once they had the accounts directly controlled by Camacho, she wanted the money to be transferred to a holding account that he had no access to, and she wanted his accounts to look normal but have only a couple of hundred dollars in them.

Johnnie asked what she would do with the money.

She said that she planned to funnel it to various charities.

He laughed and said that she was becoming the Cincinnati Robinhood.

She nodded and replied, "take from the rich crook and give to the poor and needy."

Bill came into the huddle room and said that they had been able to pull the serial number off the rifle and had the name of the last registered owner.

Alex asked Bill to talk to that owner and find out what he knew about the rifle and if he had sold it, she wanted to know who it had been sold to.

She asked about the fingerprints on the carrying case and on any of the ammo.

Bill said that they were being processed and would all end up in the database file that she had set up. There were fingerprints of someone other than the shooter, but they would have to be run to see if they were in the database.

Johnnie looked up from his computer and said he would set up a fingerprint to visual search as soon as he was done with transferring the money into Alex's charity Robin Hood account. He commented that he had the local banks and three offshore banks where Camacho had accounts. He had left only one hundred dollars in each of the local banks, and he was going to zero out the offshore banks so that there would be a very limited amount Camacho could draw on.

Alex suggested that they call it a day and that she and Johnnie would work together at his place.

She commented that she wanted to shut down the Red Bandana operation in the next day or two, but she wanted to have bullet proof evidence against Camacho and as many of his distributors as possible. She looked over at Trevor and asked if he was ready for a dirty work assignment the next day.

Trevor smiled and said he would take the dirty work if she took on the shooting work.

Alex shook her head and said that she was letting Trey take the lead because she wanted to shoot first and then ask questions afterwards.

Bill spoke up and reminded her that Trey had been asking to shoot someone so he was not sure anyone at the bar that pulled a weapon would survive.

Alex said that she was going to update the Chief, and that everyone else should go home.

Alex knocked on the Chief's door and went in when she heard him say, "Come in."

The Chief asked if she had what she needed to close the case.

Alex nodded and said that by the following afternoon she planned to shut down the Red Bandana operation. She said she would want several backup units at the bar and several out at the Meth lab. She added that she and Trey would take the bar and Bill and Trevor would take the meth lab.

The Chief said that he would arrange for the backup units to be ready to move at her command. He said that he wanted to be with Bill and Trevor.

He felt that they might face an illogical response at the lab. He smiled and said that he trusted that she would give Comacho a chance to be arrested.

She nodded and said that she would, but she added that if he pulled his weapon he wouldn't live for long because both Trey and she were in a very angry mood.

The Chief nodded and said that in either case he would have her back. He wanted to make sure everyone practiced safety first.

Alex thanked him and said it was time for her to go to her apartment and then see how Matt was doing.

Johnnie talked constantly as the two of them rode their bikes to the apartment. As they got to the elevator, he watched Alex get on and then asked how Matt was doing.

Alex replied that after she showered and cleaned up, she was going to the hospital to find out.

She got to her apartment and opened the door and almost dropped her bike when she saw Matt sitting in the recliner.

Matt smiled and said that he had convinced the Dr. who he knew quite well that his team would escort him to his apartment where he would rest and relax much better than at the hospital.

Alex put her bike on the porch and then came over and gave him a kiss. She asked if there was anything special, he wanted for dinner.

He smiled and said he wanted the Spaghetti Alfredo that he had ordered and then he wanted a hot cup of tea, a scoop of vanilla over some fresh strawberries and a hot oatmeal cookie.

Alex gave a small laugh and said he could have it all. She would go down and pick up the Alfredo when it was delivered. She asked if it was alright to invite Johnnie up because she wanted him to do some work that evening.

Matt replied that it was OK with him because he was going to sit and relax.

He added that she and Johnnie could work as long as they wanted.

10 Laying Low

The news about the shooting and the fact that his assassin was dead had Camacho focused on getting out of town. He packed his most important belongings into his Mercedes. He would leave everything else alone. He figured he could lay low for a time and then return when the heat was off.

Everything seemed to be going fine. He went into his back office to download all his files onto a thumb drive and then he was going to factory reset the computer so it would be clean. He had just withdrawn twenty thousand dollars from his accounts in order to pay the assassin and he wanted to see if he could withdraw some from another account so that he would be able to use cash instead of his credit card. When he got into his account, he was shocked to find only one hundred dollars in the account. He knew it should have had close to one hundred thousand dollars in it. Whenever an account reached one hundred thousand dollars, he would transfer the money to one of his offshore accounts. He had not transferred any money! He wondered who on his team knew about the accounts. He could not think of anyone.

In the office safe he had the money that had come in the previous day, so he had almost twenty thousand dollars and he had the ten thousand that would have been the payment for a successful hit. He opened the safe and put the money in one of his gym bags.

He factory reset his computer.

He then decided to contact his police informant to see if he could find out what was going on with the investigation into the shooting and decided it was time to leave.

His informant let him know that his Meth lab had been located and that it would be raided the following afternoon, and the bar would also be raided. His contact said that the rifle that the shooter had used was being processed and the fingerprints on the rifle and the rifle carrying case were being processed.

Camacho knew that he had not touched either, so he knew he was in the clear, but he knew that one set of fingerprints would belong to one of his lieutenants that had brought the case in and had handed it to his assassin. He thought about the rifle and knew that the serial numbers had been filed off but figured that some new sophisticated technique might pull the numbers out. That probably meant the same lieutenant whose fingerprints were on the carrying case would get connected to the purchase of the rifle at the flea market.

It was time to leave. He would clear out and figure out how and where he might start over.

Once he got to his car he looked nervously around to see if he was being watched.

He was now spooked. He wanted to go to each of his local banks to check about his accounts but if he did, he would show up on surveillance cameras. He knew that he needed to get out of town.

But driving his car on the highway was an invitation to be stopped by the highway patrol. He decided to go to his trustworthy supplier of cheap cars. This supplier was a used car lot owner that also helped distribute drugs.

He would leave his car at the lot and get a good working used car and use a temporary plate. He would pick up the Mercedes at a later date.

He had been pondering where he might go. He did not want to go to any major city where he might be made by some other drug pusher. He was not so worried about the cops because they hardly communicated within their own departments let alone with other jurisdictions.

He decided to go to a bed and breakfast in the New York State, Finger Lakes area where he had enjoyed fishing a few years ago. He could do some golfing, fishing, and hiking. He figured that by moving from one finger lake to another he could stay hidden for a substantial amount of time.

He could also get money transferred from one of the offshore accounts to a local bank so he would not have to worry about running short.

He was lucky that it was off season at the Finger Lakes. He was able to book a week at the first bed and breakfast he called. The next four went just like the first. He said that he would pay cash when he arrived and got agreement at all four.

He took his time and arrived at the first B&B in the late afternoon. He got the pick of the rooms and chose one on the top floor with a view of the lake. He asked about going fishing and was told that the B&B had a boat at the public pier, and they had the fishing tackle with the boat. It had a small electric motor that would need to be unplugged from the pier's electrical outlet. The bait had to be purchased from the bait store at the head of the pier.

Comacho figured he would do some fishing the next day.

He got the address of a local bank and planned to go there and set himself up before doing any fishing.

He sat outside on the slope of the lush green lawn and enjoyed the sunset as it went down on the other side of the lake. He was now more relaxed and felt that he would be able to survive this bump in what had otherwise been a good road.

The next morning, he drove to the local bank. He was surprised at the diminutive feel of the entrance area, but he was quickly greeted and then ushered into a private room when he said he wanted to set up an account.

He had a fake passport, the account number, and the bank routing number for the offshore account he was planning to get the money. He asked to have four thousand dollars transferred into the account he was setting up.

After setting up the account, the bank manager said that she was ready to transfer the money in. He gave her the account and routing number. After a few moments she looked at him and said that the message from the bank stated that the account had been closed the previous day.

Comacho had to control his facial features. He had no clue how the account could have been closed. He smiled, apologized, and said that his accountant must not have had time to notify him about having closed it.

He looked in his walled and pulled out a card that had the account and routing number for another bank.

The bank manager put the transfer request in and a few moments later shook her head and said that she got the same response as the first bank.

He was now in a state of alarm.

He pulled out another card and gave her the numbers.

The result was the same.

He was now in total shock. He found it hard not to scream.

He asked how much he needed to deposit to open the account.

The manager said that one dollar would open the account, but it would not allow any withdrawal of monies.

He opened his wallet and took out four fifty-dollar bills and put it on the desk. He said he would deposit more in the next couple days as soon as he talked to his accountant.

He shook his head and said that he was going to give his accountant a call and read him the riot act for not letting him know what was going on.

He was in a daze as he walked out of the bank and got into his car and drove away. He drove to the fishing pier, bought some bait, a beer, sandwich, and a cap with the words, "Finger Lakes" over the blue finger lake background.

Camacho went through putting the bait on the hook, casting, and slowly reeling in the line as he sat staring in a mental haze. The three banks had close to seventy-five million dollars each that was his personal nest egg. He kept the operating money in his office safe and was constantly paying out for more drugs and paying each of his distributors with that money. That money flowed smoothly and periodically he could skim some off and put it in his offshore accounts.

He had no open accountants. He had never given any of the offshore information to anyone in his operation. He had always thought that the offshore banks were ultra-safe. He wondered how someone could have zeroed out the accounts.

He looked around and when he knew he was the only one within ear shot he let out a blood curling scream. He wanted to put somebody into a barrel of lye.

Johnnie let Alex know that he had found Camacho's home address and car registration and license number for his Mercedes.

As soon as she had the home address, she asked the Chief to dispatch two units to watch the house and make sure no one left while she was at the bar.

She reminded the Chief about everyone having their protective gear on.

He chuckled and said that Trevor had reminded him to be wearing his Kevlar.

She then asked if Johnnie wanted to have a quick lunch before she had the raids begin.

He shook his head and said that he was running the fingerprints on the rifle carrying case and on the barrel of the rifle. He figured knowing the identity of this person might be useful before the raid.

Alex nodded and said she would have his favorite pizza delivered. She took the information on the Mercedes and put out an APB while she waited for the pizza delivery.

Trey commented that if Comacho had left town he doubted he would drive his personal car.

Alex looked over to Johnnie who was sitting and relaxing. She asked if he had a hit on the search.

Johnnie shook his head and added that he had launched an automated search application that allowed him to relax.

Alex smiled and said that he continued to surprise her. She sat down and tried to relax.

The pizza arrived and as soon as they each had taken a bite the search engine rang a bell.

Johnnie flashed the picture and name of the person that was a match to the fingerprints. He sent the picture to the team.

Alex thanked Johnnie and said that as soon as they were done with lunch, she would trigger the raids.

After lunch, Alex called the Chief and let him know that he should let all units know to it was time for the raids.

He said that he, Bill, and Trevor were in position, but he had arranged for the two units that had led several previous Meth lab raids to take the lead. They had double respirators and goggles and had issued the three of them sets that they were to wear. They had suggested that we stake the exterior in case any of the folks inside jumped out of windows. They had also given each of them thin rubber gloves to wear. He said that he was glad he had let them take the lead.

Alex replied that she was glad that he had put them in charge and wished them luck.

Trey had been listening and commented that he was glad they had taken on the bar.

Alex led the way out of the station and walked toward the bar. She saw the two units parked ahead of them and gave them a call and let them know she was approaching on foot.

The four got out and greeted her.

She verified that they had their armor and head gear with them. She asked that two of them take the rear entrance to the bar and two the front of the bar.

She let them know that she and Trevor would go in. If they heard any shooting, they were to enter with guns drawn ready to fire. She did not want them to shoot her or Trey by mistake.

One of the younger policemen smiled and said that they would make sure not to since he had heard that every person that had taken a shot at her was dead.

Alex smiled and said the dead ones all had hit her or had made the mistake of trying to.

She then pointed to the bar and said they should get into position.

She led the way to the front door and stepped in and to the right as Trevor stepped in behind her and stepped to the left.

The several screens were playing scenes of various sports games but were silent. The lights were bright, and the walls were decorated with pictures of a variety of famous baseball and football players.

She shouted out that it was the police, and no one should move except to put their hands in the air.

The bar tender put his hands up as did the two guys sitting in one of the booths.

Alex watched as the person at the bar reached into his jacket and began to turn his left side toward Trey and her. She shot him in his right arm triceps muscle.

He screamed out that she had shot him in the back.

Alex said that it was the back of his arm, and he was lucky to be alive.

The four officers rushed in, and hand cuffed the other three as Alex and Trey handled the person she had shot.

She addressed the person she had shot by his name and said that he was under arrest as an accomplice to the attempted assassination of a police officer.

Trey read him his Miranda rights as he handcuffed his left arm to the bar foot rail. He stepped away as the EMT team entered with some additional police.

Eli, the person that had been shot said he had nothing to do with the shooting.

Alex told him to save his breath and tell his story to the judge.

She asked one of the older officers who she could leave in charge to handle the situation and after making sure that the person she had arrested was taken care of she said that she was going to leave the scene because she was going to a raid at another site.

She said that the bullet she had fired had hit the bar and skip over and had hit one of the bottles of liquor on the other side somewhere near the last three bottles.

She put her weapon in an evidence bag and handed it to him.

He asked what she wanted to do with the other three.

She told him to check them out and if they had any tickets to arrest them and hold them for as long as was legal.

The officer said he had the crime scene under control and would get the details about the raid of the bar from her when she was back from the other raid.

Alex led the way out and she and Trey walked back to where her car was parked. She asked Trey to drive.

The call she was expecting came in. It was Trevor calling.

Trevor said that Bill had shot some crazy guy wearing double filter breathers and goggles that had jumped out the window shooting at them and yes, the guy was dead.

He said that the people inside were all being escorted out and placed on the ground in the fire station parking lot. He said that the three of them were done and ready to leave.

Alex gave him the address where she and Trey were going and asked if the three of them could join her.

She heard the Chief reply that they were on the way and that she should wait for them and that he had already been informed that she was weaponless.

Alex chuckled and said that she had borrowed Matt's weapon that he had gladly loaned her.

Trey spoke up loudly that it was his turn to do the shooting.

They waited for the Chief and as soon as everyone was ready, Alex, Trey, and the Chief took the front, Bill and Trevor had the back and the four other officers had the two sides of the house.

Trey took the lead and after the house had been cleared and when it was certain that no one was in the house Alex asked that they search the place to see if they could figure out where Camacho might have gone.

Bill said he knew the routine and began looking for picture albums.

Alex got a call from Johnnie who let her know that he was at the bar and was examining the two computers that were part of the internal network. He let her know that the one in the back office had been factory reset but he had located that back up that was always done by the reset routine, and he had downloaded that to his computer. He said that he would soon have all the information about the operation. He chuckled and said that he had done everything in a legal and above way and all his information could be used in court.

Alex told him that he had just earned a special lunch and a tray of cookies.

Johnnie laughed and said that he loved working with her, but she should stop trying to fatten him up.

Trevor spoke up and said he thought he had where Camacho might have gone. He held up a picture that had Camacho holding up a pole with a large fish still on the line and he had the middle finger of his right hand prominently displayed. He said the back of the picture was dated a few years ago and the words "caught on a fly on the middle Finger Lake."

Alex asked Johnnie if he had heard what Trevor had just said.

Johnnie replied that he had, and he was on it. He said he would search the hotels and B&Bs to see if they had any recent single men check in.

Alex suggested that they repeat their work session in her apartment. She would check with Matt about what he wanted for dinner and get that set up. She suggested a seven PM start.

11 Finger Lakes

Rose-Anne was shocked when she heard that Matt had been shot as he saved Alex from getting assassinated. She had been sure that this request for help would not be a threat to either of them. She was about to apologize when Alex told her not to say it.

Alex had called her mother to let her know about the attempted assassination and that the assassin was dead and she was on the trail of the person who she thought had hired him. She assured her mother that both Matt and her would be fine.

Rose-Anne suggested that the two of them come up and relax and go fishing.

Alex said that she would talk it over with Matt and that she would let her know later about going fishing.

That had been a few days ago.

Since then, the raids had taken place, and she was certain that it was only a matter of time before she would have Camacho under arrest.

She and Johnnie set themselves up to work at her kitchen table. They first feasted on some ribs that Matt had ordered in. Johnnie thanked Matt for picking one of his favorite meals and he hoped he would be able to stay awake long enough to figure out where in the Finger Lake area Camacho was staying.

Matt laughed and said he had ordered the ribs because he planned to fall asleep while they worked into the night.

Alex sat on the recliner arm as she ate one of the ribs and then gave Matt a barbecue sauce kiss and thanked him for being so gracious.

Matt laughed and licked his lips and said it was the sweetest kiss that he had gotten from her in a long time.

She suggested that while Johnnie was searching for the needle in the haystack in the Finger Lakes, she would make a batch of cookies and then serve them with vanilla ice cream topped with fresh strawberries and some whipped yogurt.

Johnnie said that he thought she had a great idea. He focused on linking first with the B&Bs and getting into their computer hubs to get to their guest registers. He got the addresses of all he B&Bs on the central Finger Lake. He hoped that Comacho would return to the place in the picture. That would greatly shorten the search. He put his automated hacking software to work and then sat back and picked on the remains of the dinner.

Alex asked how he was approaching the search and after listening to Johnnie's explanation said that his approach made a lot of sense.

She had made cookies so many times that she could do it blindfolded. As she took out the tray of oatmeal raisin cookies from the oven, Johnnie exclaimed that he thought he might have where Comacho was staying. The reservation had been called in about the time Comacho would have been leaving Cincinnati. The transaction was to have been in cash.

Johnnie commented that now it would take good old fashioned shoe leather to verify that it was actually Camacho.

Alex smiled and asked Matt if he wanted to come along to the Finger Lakes.

She took out three bowls and scooped out some vanilla ice cream, added a half a dozen fresh strawberries to each bowl and then put on a scoop of yogurt and topped off with honey. She put a spoon in each bowl and passed them out.

She sat down facing Matt and asked if he felt good enough to ride to the Finger Lakes. They could rent a room and relax there for several days.

Johnnie said that he could drive Matt up after she and Trey captured Camacho.

Alex shook her head and said that she planned to bring Camacho back to Cincinnati and then return afterwards with Matt if the place met her expectations.

Matt said that a stay in the Finger Lake area would be a great way to use his recovery time.

Alex looked at the time and decided it was still early enough to let Trey know about their drive to the Finger Lakes area. She asked Johnnie how far it was to the middle lake.

Johnnie said that the middle lake and the B&B were about five hundred miles by car.

Alex thought for a minute and then called Trey and let him know about the drive to the Finger Lakes and that he should come prepared to spend the night. They would drive up, arrest Camacho, and then drive back the next day.

After hanging up with Trey she called the Chief to update him. She verified that she would be able to use the department's prisoner transport van. She also asked him to contact the sheriff of Aurora, New York and give him a heads-up about the situation and her intentions of bringing Camacho back to Cincinnati.

The Chief complimented her on finding Camacho and said she could have the van and he would contact the sheriff.

Alex thanked him and said she would see him in the morning before leaving.

She then asked Johnnie what else they should be doing before she got up there.

Johnnie said that he was not sure that he could think of anything else.

He smiled and said that he would make sure that Matt got a good lunch and dinner the next day.

Alex nodded and said that she felt much better about the fact that Matt would have someone to look after him.

Matt said that if it weren't for the bandages and the sling he would go for a bike ride, but he said that he preferred to eat out for lunch and dinner because it would give him a chance to do some walking.

Johnnie nodded and said he would be glad to walk with him to make sure that if he fell, he would have someone to pick him up.

Matt laughed and said he had been shot in the shoulder and his legs were just fine.

Alex asked Matt about the need to change the bandages.

Matt said that his team was dropping by the next day in the afternoon to redo the bandages and reduce their size. He was hoping for a big band aid on each side of the wound if it was not oozing. He figured he would have to keep using the arm sling for a couple of more days.

Johnnie cleared the table, closed his laptop, and said that he was going back to his apartment.

Alex said that she would ride in on her own and leave her bike at the station.

Johnnie shook his head and said that he would ride in with her and then she could bring him and the two bikes back to the apartment, get her suitcase and then go on to the Finger Lakes with Trey.

Alex said that was a great plan. She would meet him at the elevators in the morning.

The next morning, she walked into the office to find Bill and Trevor sitting with suitcases by their desk. She asked where they were going.

Trevor handed her half of a bear claw and said that he understood that she was sponsoring an overnight at the Finger Lakes and he and Bill did not want to miss out.

Alex smiled and asked if the Chief had called them.

Bill nodded and said that the Chief had more or less ordered them to go with her. He had said that Comacho might be very angry at being taken down and might get violent.

Alex took a bite of her Bear Claw, a sip of her coffee and walked to the Chief's office and knocked on the door.

The Chief called out for her to come in.

Alex thanked him for inviting Bill and Trevor but asked if he thought it was necessary.

The Chief replied that the last time he had let her, and Trey go alone on a drug case Trey had ended up near death and she had killed four gangsters.

She again thanked him and said she would keep him linked in.

She left and as she stepped out, she saw that Trey had arrived and was eating his half of the bear claw and joking with Johnnie.

She came over and asked who wanted to drive first.

Trevor said he would be glad to.

She pointed to the exit and said that it was time to get going.

They stopped to drop Johnnie off.

She took her bike up to her apartment and got her suitcase.

Matt wished her a good trip and then she left.

She put her suitcase in with the other three and then got into the seat behind Trevor.

After each hour they changed drivers, they stopped for a sit-down lunch and then continued. They stopped at a family restaurant for dinner.

Alex called ahead and made reservations at a B&B near where Camacho was staying. She planned to arrest him the following morning and then drive back to Cincinnati.

She let everyone know that she wanted to be at the B&B where Camacho was staying when he came down for breakfast. So, they would need to be out at his B&B at about five thirty.

The next morning the four of them drove the short distance to the B&B.

Alex asked Bill and Trevor to stake out the back of the house and Trey should take the front. She was going in to speak to whomever was preparing breakfast.

She walked in and made her way to the kitchen where she introduced herself, showed her badge and asked if she had a guest name Comacho.

The proprietress said she had only one guest at the moment, but his name was Hank.

Alex pulled out Camacho's picture and showed it to her.

Yes, that's Hank was the immediate response.

Alex asked if he had come down for breakfast yet.

"He went out early to do some fishing," was the reply. She went on to say that he asked her to hold his breakfast and he might bring in a fish for lunch.

Alex asked her if she could see Hank's room. When she looked in through the open door of the room, she commented that it had a great view of the lake. She walked to the window, and she could see Camacho fishing.

She looked around and saw a duffel bag tucked under the edge of the bed. She wanted to look inside but did not have a search warrant, so she walked out of the room.

She thanked the proprietress and said that she would wait for Hank out by the pier.

She walked out the front and asked Trey to get Bill and Trevor. She walked to the corner of the house and watched as Camacho caught a nice large bass.

She pointed out where Camacho was sitting in his boat then asked Bill and Travis to move the police van out of sight and then come back.

Alex moved behind a large old oak with limbs spread out as if to shield those standing below them. She had Trey stand behind a similar tree on the other side of the dock.

Bill and Trevor had returned and were standing at the corner of the house.

Trevor waved at her and held up his gun.

Camacho figured that one large fish was all he needed for lunch, so he took the boat in, brought it along the pier, and tied it off. He got all the stuff out of the boat and plug the battery in. He held the bass about the size of his forearm with a finger in its gills and carried the rest of his gear with his right arm.

When he got to the end of the pier and as he passed the bait shop and was approaching the tree that Alex was standing behind, she stepped out and declared that he was under arrest and should put everything down and raise his hands in the air.

Camacho dropped everything and drew his gun and got one shot off.

Alex had anticipated the reaction and had stepped to the right as she pulled her weapon and shot him three times.

Three other shots rang out at almost the same time.

Camacho was surprised at the speed of her actions, but he never got to think about anything else because his world went black. It took his body a moment to realize it was dead and fall to the ground.

Alex walked over to his body and moved his gun aside with her toe.

The proprietress came out the back door where Bill stopped her.

She looked at him and said that the Black detective seemed to be such a sweet person.

Bill replied that she was until someone shot at her then she was deadlier than a rattlesnake with babies to defend.

Alex called the Chief and informed him of what had happened and asked him to call the local sheriff and inform him about the situation and that she needed a legal search warrant to go through Camacho's room and personal stuff.

She suggested that the Chief arrange to have Comacho's body sent back to Cincinnati so the coroner could do his job. She asked if the lot of them would need to leave their weapons as part of the evidence. She let him know that if they got done in time they would drive back to Cincinnati.

She then walked back to where Bill was standing with the proprietress and apologized for them having had to shoot Hank, but he had shot at her first and they had all responded.

The proprietress asked what Hank was wanted for.

Alex explained that Hank was a drug dealer known as Camacho. He had hired and assassin to kill an officer of the law. He also operated a drug production operation that had been shut down.

The proprietress shook her head and said that he had seemed to be a nice person. He had talked about setting himself up to live in the area and had even asked about where he could find a trustworthy bank.

Alex asked about what bank that might be. Once she got the name, she sent it to Johnnie and said that she would deposit any money found in the bag that Camacho had in his room into that account and then later Johnnie could transfer it to the Robin Hood account and zero out the one at the at the Finger Lake bank.

Bill let the proprietress know that the sheriff was coming with a search warrant so they could legally search the room that Comacho had rented.

He asked if she would serve them lunch. He assured her that they would pay whatever she decided to charge them.

When Alex heard him making the request she walked over to where the fish was still flopping and picked it up and carried it to where the proprietress was standing and said that a fish for lunch would be great.

The proprietress took the fish and said she would put it in the oven with some small potatoes and cut carrots around it and bake it.

Alex asked if a room with a good view was available for the rest of the week.

The proprietress laughed and said that one had just come open.

Alex said she would take it for at least five days.

12 Middle Finger...Lake !

Alex's return to Cincinnati was anticlimactic. The Chief congratulated her and asked what she had planned. She let him know that she was taking vacation and returning to the Finger Lakes with Matt to do some fishing and just relax. She let him know that she would drop off her official case report in the morning.

The Chief suggested that she send it in with Johnnie and save herself a trip.

Later that day, she and Matt agreed that they would take their time driving to the Lake. They planned on one stop at about the halfway point on the way up. They both had enough vacation and they had decided to spend a full seven days on the Lake.

She called her mother and let her know that she was going to vacation and fish in the Middle Finger Lake.

He Mother joked about getting the middle finger treatment.

Alex laughed and replied that was not the case, but she and Matt had decided to fish in a new lake.

Alex stayed just at the speed limit which was uncharacteristic for her. She usually drove a few miles over the limit but for this trip she had decided to relax and that to her meant staying at the speed limit when driving.

During the halfway stop, the two of them ordered room service and watched a movie with a happy story.

When they arrived at the B&B, Evon, the proprietress, greeted them and then said that she needed to apologize but she had advertised that she was hosting a world-famous detective from Cincinnati known as "Cincinnati's Black Annie Oakley" and the B&B was fully booked. She said that she had six guests from Cincinnati and several from around Ohio.

Alex laughed and asked if she could reserve the fishing boat for each morning so she and Matt could get their fishing in.

Evon said that she had arranged to have enough boats for everyone that wanted to go out would have their own boat. She said that this surge was going to keep her business afloat for another year. She asked if what she had done was OK with Alex.

Alex said that it was not and that it would cost Evon a free dinner with the fish she and Matt would bring in.

Evon smiled and said that she would even clean the fish and prepare it any way that Alex wanted.

Alex asked about Mom-and-Pop restaurants that might offer great meals.

Evon said she would make a list of the places that were within walking distance and those that might be a drive but worth it.

Two days into the vacation, Alex got a call from the Chief. He let her know that all of those arrested had court dates during the coming few days. He let her know that he and the rest of the team would cover the arraignments and she did not need to be there. He wondered about the fact that Camacho' business showed a zero balance in the one bank account that was still open.

Alex replied that as one of his last acts Camacho had opened a charity called, "Open Hands to all Needing Help." He had given it close to three hundred million dollars.

The Chief laughed and said that he was sorry that Camacho was no longer around to get the praise he deserved for being so kind and generous.

Alex replied in a serious tone that she had been deeply depressed after she realized that the team had shot and killed such a nice guy.

The Chief told her to get over it and to enjoy the fishing and he would see her when she got back.

The fishing was good and every day the two of them would bring several fish in and give them to Evon.

Evon asked if she could prepare the fish and serve them to her guests.

Alex said that she could do whatever she wanted with the fish. She added that they had eaten all the fish that they had wanted to. She added that she and Matt were planning to enjoy the T-bone that she had on her menu for that evening.

During the week Alex was approached numerous times by the guests and asked for her autograph.

Matt commented that he felt like he was out with a superstar.

She was pleased that Matt had healed well and no longer needed to wear his sling. She helped him rebandage the bullet wound and was pleased that it had only left a small entrance scar and a larger but clean exit scar.

On their last day both of them caught their limit. Alex picked out five of the largest fish and she and Matt cleaned them and put them in a cooler in the ice. She planned to give one to each of the team.

Evon thanked them for their stay and let Alex know that the ads she had placed in several of the B&B magazines and the ones online were all generating additional bookings. She invited both of them back whenever they wanted to enjoy some more fishing.

Alex thanked her and wished her well.

She and Matt left after breakfast and did the drive back in one day. This time Matt insisted that they share the driving.

Alex stopped by Johnnie's apartment and gave him his fish and asked how things had been going.

Johnnie replied that it had been going slow, but he thought he might have a case that she should look into.

Alex put up her hand and told him to enjoy the fish, but she did not want to hear about a potential case because she still had a mark on her chest where she had been shot on the last special case, he had brought up.

Johnnie thanked her for the fish and then reminded her that the kids that she had saved now called her Aunt Alex.

Alex gave Johnnie a hug, said goodnight and then left.

Matt had waited at the elevator and the two rode up together and walked down to their apartment.

Matt let her know that while she was talking to Johnnie, he had gotten a call to verify that he would be at the curb a five in the morning to be picked up.

Alex nodded and said that shortly after that she would be riding in to work with Johnnie.

The following morning Johnnie was at the elevator. He was eager to let Alex know about a potential case that he had run across by accident. He figured she would be the one that would solve such a mystery.

Alex knew immediately that she was going to be listening to Johnnie about his potential case. She told him that she did not want to hear a thing about a new case until everything connected with the current case was complete.

She added that her goal for that day was to hand out the fish that were in the cooler she was strapping to her bike.

Johnnie smiled and replied that she was missing out on a really interesting twist to a case that had gone unsolved for many years and that he was sure she would get hooked as soon as she heard the details of the case.

Alex put on her helmet and said that it would be at least a week before she would be willing to hear what he wanted to tell her.

The End

Preview of: The Shadow Fighter

The Shots that Should Have

*L*orenzo was up early as he had planned. The stars were still twinkling overhead as he walked across the square to the elevator that would take him down to sub level four. The beads of sweat on his forehead made it clear to him that it was going to be a very warm humid day. He hoped that he would be able to find a shady spot on the roof that he would be lying on.

He moved his car from the basement parking area to street parking near the exit to the River Front Park. He walked along the old rail tracks and then crossed through the pine trees and after checking that no one was around he climbed up on the roof of what he had realized was the park's maintenance building. The sun was just rising, and the day was just beginning to heat up, but he already could feel the humidity climbing. He pulled the bill of his cap down. He hoped that the opportunity for a good shot would be available quickly because as he looked around the roof he was going to be totally exposed to the rising sun.

He stood the old wooden pallet that had been abandoned on the roof on edge so that a shadow was created in the area that he was going to be lying.

He was trying to keep the black surface of the roof as cool as he possibly could. He rolled out his exercise mat that acted like an insulator.

He once again sighted through the scope to make certain he had the position that he wanted. He then lay down to wait. He would have liked to go for a walk, but he did not want to risk being seen climbing up or down from the roof. He accepted the waiting because it was a very common part of his job. He lay down, put his hat over his eyes, and took a nap.

He came awake to the music from a band warming up. He looked over the edge of the roof and saw that people were arriving and staking out their spots on the grassy hill in front of the band stand structure. He saw that many of them had beach umbrellas up. He wished he could have one where he was.

He saw that the concession stand was already doing good business handing out water, soft drinks, coffee, and rolls. He was able to read the menu sign and was impressed that everything was free of charge. He chuckled to himself as he got the urge to go down and get coffee and a roll.

He read the sign in front of the larger tent that invited everyone in for a free showing of *Annie L. Scots*, many Scapes scenes and it added that on exit each person could select a miniature picture of the Scape scene that they liked best.

The second thing that caught his eye was the donation station for an organization called "Young Women's Helping Hands" that offered a second Scape picture for a donation of any amount.

He wondered how any persons associated with the scene below had earned Adriano's ire. It was not something that bothered him, but it did make him wonder because these seemed to be people that he would have wanted to have back in Sicily.

He finally spotted his target as she walked out to look down to where the first band was now playing. He waited until she turned around. He was just pulling very slowly on the trigger when suddenly she was pushed from behind into the tent. He managed to pull his finger off the trigger. He waited for just a second then decided that he had somehow been discovered and decided that it was time to abandon his assassination attempt and make his way to his car slowly but as fast as possible and leave the area. He would try again on another day from another location.

Trey had been following his normal routine when he and Alex were out in public. He was always slightly behind and on one side and at the ready. He was about to ask her if she wanted something to drink when he spotted the laser spot on her back. His reflexes took over and he pushed her as hard as he could into the tent and followed her in. He had expected to get hit but nothing happened.

Alex was surprised at the strength of the push that hurled her through the entrance flap and caused her to stumble and fall just short of hitting the first painting pedestal. She jumped up and reflexively pulled her weapon. Trey put up his hands up.

Alex looked around to see if they had scared anyone and she put her weapon away. He told her about the laser beam. They both cautiously lifted the entrance flap and walked out along the side that was covered. There was only one close by building. They decided to check it out. Both of them would have preferred to have their weapons at the ready but that would have scared the people still arriving for the concert.

They circled around back of what they realized was the park maintenance building and cautiously approached the steel ladder going to the roof. Trey pointed at it and indicated that he was going up and that she should take a few steps back to provide him cover. Once he got to the top of the ladder, he cautiously looked over it and then wave her to come up.

Alex went up and they walked over to where a sniper's rifle and ammunition had been abandoned.

Alex called in to the dispatch center and asked that an investigative team come to investigate the scene of an attempted assassination. She gave the location and instructed those coming to the scene to refrain from using sirens or flashing lights.

She and Trey climbed down from the roof and stood by waiting.

Johnnie had been out by the concession stand flying Gunjfor taking pictures of the crowd when he observed Trey pushing Alex into the tent and following her in. He immediately took Gunjfor up and turned it slowly around and caught someone on the roof of the nearest building crawling to the fire escape in the back.

He took Gunjfor swooping in for a close up but had to pull up to avoid the pine trees. From a higher vantage point, he spotted the person that had left the roof get into a car in the parking lot. He flew Gunjfor toward that location. He was able to get the direction that the car was heading and figured that a quick call to central might get a unit to cut him off and apprehend the person trying to get away.

He brought Gunjfor down and then walked to where he had seen Alex and Trey going.

They were just coming down from the roof when he got there.

Alex looked at him and asked if by chance he had been able to get anything with Gunjfor.

Johnnie smiled, shook his head, and said that he had the backside of the shooter and the back side of the getaway car, but he did not have much else but behinds of some person and that person's car. The licensed plate had a grey cover that hid the license plate.

Alex asked to see what Johnnie had captured. As she watched the video, she said that she wanted to get the information to the lab so that the photo analysts could do an in-depth detailed analysis. She said that the shoes, the shirt, and pants might all hold a clue as to who that person might be. She pointed to the license plate that had a grey cover that seemed make the license plate unreadable but perhaps the analysist might be able to see through it. The rear of the car had no auto make emblems, so she figured the shooter was a professional.

Johnnie got on line and sent the footage to the lab. Then he said that he was going back to filming the event.

Alex thanked Trey for literally having her back and gave him a hug.

Trey nodded and said that it was not often that he got the opportunity to shove her around. He then said that he was ready to enjoy the rest of the day with Nolan and Lesley.

Alex asked where they were.

Trey said that when he shoved her into the tent they were walking and looking at the Scape paintings. He added that Lesley had observed what had happened and had guided Nolan to the back of the tent. He figured he would have to explain the situation to them.

Alex shook her head and commented that she had no idea why she was on someone's hit list.

Trey laughed and replied that she had left a trail of bodies, people in prison and destroyed gunships and burned down coal barges that left a huge number of potential people mad enough that they might think about trying to do her in.

Alex said that she agreed that there was a long trail but that he was exaggerating the number of people left alive to try to get revenge.

Trey agreed and said that no one came to mind.

Alex said that it was similar to the Scape scene Annie had captured of what she called the Alex Scape painting that was featured as the first painting when a person entered the display tent. That was a case where a racist had decided to kill her because her skin color offended him.

Lindsey was standing pointing to the picture of the Scape that featured their backyard. It was of Nolan, Linda, and Laurie on the swing set. This was a painting that she had purchased during Alex's private showing of Annie's Scapes when Alex had hosted a party for all her friends. She was thrilled to be able to get a painting of the time several years ago when the kids were younger. The three kids were now at least six or seven years older and no longer children but young adults.

She saw Alex fly in and sprawl on the floor and immediately jump up with her weapon pulled. She watched as Trey followed her in. Alex immediately put her weapon away and the two of them cautiously left the tent.

She guided Nolan to the back of the tent expecting gunfire but there was none. She continued guiding Nolan around to take in all the different Scapes that Annie had painted.

She was hesitant to leave the tent and engaged Annie in conversation.

Trey returned and saw that Lindsey was still in the tent. He walked over and asked if she was ready to go sit out on the lawn and listen to the music.

She asked what had happened.

Trey responded that nothing had happened and that was a good thing. He said that he would share more once he knew more.

Nolan laughed and said now he understood why he had been kept in the tent. He then added that he was ready for something to drink, something to snack on, and he wanted to listen to the bands that Linda and Lorie had chosen for the event.

Trey took Lindsey's hand and led the way out.

Brian had been in the tent watching Annie as she walked around and engaged the people looking at her paintings. He had observed Alex as she flew in and landed at the base of the first picture. He remained seated but was ready to act if necessary. He called to Kekoa who was out on the lawn with Anela and asked if there was anything strange going on. He listened as Kekoa replied that things were calm, and the only action was on the stage. Kekoa added that the two girls had done a great job in selecting the first opening group.

Brian had noticed Lindsey's reaction, so he walked over and talked to her and Nolan. He knew that Annie considered Lindsey a good friend and the two girls still argued in fun as to who got to marry Nolan.

It seemed like quite a while before Alex and Trey returned but it was clear to him that they had things in control.

He walked over to Annie and asked if he could get her anything.

Lorenzo made his way to the highway and drove north. He was keeping his speed just below the speed limit and staying to the right most lane. He was thinking about what he needed to do. He definitely needed to find a place to stay for the night. It needed to be an out of the way place where he could get something to eat and hopefully buy a different car. He needed to shed all connection with his stay in Cincinnati.

He hoped to circle back and get a second chance at what he had been hired to do.

He drove until a sign loaded with fast food places and another that highlighted a number of hotels caught his eye. He figured that it was time to get something to eat and then get a room for the night and get some sleep.

In the morning after a quick breakfast, he drove around the area and found a used car lot that seemed to have a good offering of cars for sale. He found a car that seemed to be in good shape, and he traded in his current vehicle for the car plus a thousand dollars more.

He knew that the dealer was getting a good deal and if he had been in Italy, he would have bargained for a better deal for himself. He decided that he would rather get a different car and leave a happy dealer versus one that felt pressured to make the exchange.

He did not want to be remembered.

He called in to Adriano and let him know what had happened. He shared that he was returning to Cincinnati to finish the job, but he needed another sniper's rifle.

Adriano was surprised by the call but pleased that Lorenzo was planning to finish the job. He let Lorenzo know where he could pick up another sniper's rifle. He asked when he should expect the news of the targets demise.

Lorenzo replied that he was going to spend the day deciding on a new location for his next assassination attempt. He wanted a location that gave him a great shot and an easy escape. The location would depend on his targets movement.

He spent the next couple of days observing his target's morning and evening transit to and from work. She had a route down the steep hill from her home to a transit area where she crossed the highway and then rode past an apartment building where she was joined by an older bicycler who then took the lead. The route down to the apartment building was consistent but the route from there to the police station varied randomly on each of his observations.

He decided that the best place for the shot was as she came down the steep hill and crossed on the road over the highway.

He then spent time identifying the best location that would give him a good shot and an easy get away. He decided that the best location was as she got to the bottom of the hill and was getting ready to cross over the US 71 highway.

He found a way to take the service elevator to the roof. There he found a good spot and set everything up.

On Tuesday morning Alex departed from her house and rode slowly down the steep hill that took her to the point where she crossed over US 71 to get into the downtown. She loved where her house was located and the great view it provided but the way to work was a challenge and she was currently replacing her bicycle brake pads once a week because she had to engage them almost continuously to get safely down the hill.

She was crossing the bridge when a careless driver put her so close to the wall that she had to brake and push herself off the wall to keep from going over the side. As she did so the head tube of the bike shattered. As she went over her handle bar she rolled and drew her weapon. She came up behind a car stopped for the red light. She looked up at the buildings on the other side. She saw a glint. She moved immediately to her right and heard the bullet hit the cement behind her. She took three shots. One at the glint and two on either side of the glint. At the range and the upward angle, she was shooting she was not sure she had chosen the correct angle.

The stop light turned green, and she jogged along with the cars as they made the left turn at the light. She then ran across the intersection and to the base of the building. She stopped at the entrance and called in a shot fired, and an officer needing backup and gave the address. The sirens and the flashing lights of the approaching police cars were visible in less than two minutes.

Alex explained the situation and that the shooter had been on the roof, but she was not sure where he might be at the moment.

She watched as the Chief accompanied by Trey and Johnnie got out of his car and came over to her.

She pointed to where her bike was laying at the side by the wall of the road and said that was where she had first encountered being shot at and that there was another point about fifteen feet in front of that where the second bullet hit the wall.

The Chief called one of the police officers and asked him to tape of the area along the bridge that was part of the crime scene but to keep traffic flowing.

He then asked if she was OK.

Alex nodded and replied that she was going to have a few sore spots from having rolled over her handle bar, but her helmet and pads had saved her.

Johnnie had launched Gunjfor and made her fly to the top of the building. He then showed everyone where the shooter happened to be. The picture showed a large hole in the back of a person's head.

Gunjfor had arrived just as a squad of officers came across the roof with their guns drawn. One of them waved to the camera and gave a thumbs up as he pointed to the body lying face down.

Johnnie kept Gunjfor hovering until Dr Rogers arrived and gave his thumbs up while his team took pictures before he turned the dead shooter over.

He then loudly commented that only a person who shot out bull's eyes blindfolded could do the kind of shooting with the kind of results that he was seeing.

Alex said that it was time she got a ride into work and walked towards the Chief's car.

He stopped her and threw his keys to her and said that when the site was totally in control, he would re-turn to the office, and they should discuss the case. He wanted to find out who was behind the current attempts on her life.

Thank you for reading this far.

Go to Remwriter95.net to finish the story.

www.remwriter95.net/

About the Author

Ronald E. Mueller
remwriter95@gmail.com

Ron grew up in what is now Flint River State Park in Southeast Iowa. The 170-year-old house Ron lived in is built into a hillside. It faces a 125-foot-high cliff towering over the little Flint River. The house and the land talked to him about; the passing of time, the struggle to conquer the land, the struggles people faced and the wonder of nature.

He climbed the cliffs, crawled into the caves, dove from the swimming rock, collected clams from the bottom of the pond, gigged and skinned frogs for their legs. He trapped muskrats for fur, hunted raccoon in the dead of night, and with only a stick hunted rabbits in the dead of winter.

His young life was outdoors, and nature tested him.

He walked to a one room stone schoolhouse uphill both ways. A stern but warm-hearted teacher, Mrs. Henry was instrumental in shaping his character as she shepherded him from the fourth to the eighth grade.

It was a great way to grow up.

Ron graduated from Burlington, High School, went to Vietnam in the Navy. He graduated from The University of South Florida with a master's degree in engineering, worked for thirty eight years for Procter and Gamble, traveled around the world thirty times.

He has remained happily married for more than fifty years. His daughter and his two sons are all successful and his three grandchildren have all graduated.

His wife has humored and supported him as he became a full time professional story teller.

He has come to realize that he is, what is known as, a Cozy writer. Excitement and adventure but little guts and gore. His heroine or hero suffer a little but live happily ever after.

His experiences inter-twined with snippets of fantasy lend themselves to the adventures he leads the reader through.

His experiences inter-twined with snippets of fantasy lend themselves to the adventures he leads the reader through.

Books by the Author

<u>Fiction Series</u>
The Alex Evercrest Series
The River Front
The Girl on The Grill
Missing
Maggot
Racist
Votive Candles
Windy City
Country Road
Pool of Blood
Sins of the Daughter
Body Parts
The Skull Collector
The Vanishing
The Shadow Fighter
Moonshine
Grief's Trajectory
The Magic Touch
Northern Lights
Alex Evercrest Heroine
Alex Evercrest Collection Two
New Direction
A Family Affair
Disruption
The St. Lebuinnus Church Murder

A Brian O'Neil Novel
Hawaiian Phoenix
Moon Curser
Death Broker

The Problem Solver Series
Solutions
Drug Lords
Border Crosser
The Problem Solver Collection

<u>The Taelo Series</u>
Taelo: The Early Years
Taelo: The Golden Feather
Taelo: Journey of Discovery
Taelo: Dangerous Passage
Taelo: Condor Clan Slingers
Taelo: Circumvention
Taelo: The Journey of Sages
Taelo: Collection
Taelo: Future Leaders Journey

<u>A Taelo Story:</u>
White Swan and Quiet Pheasant
The Child's Name
Floating Cloud
Quiet Rabbit
Busy Bee
Little Otter & Talking Wren

Broken Spear
Burley Bear & Meadow Flower
Taelo Story Collection

Science Fiction

The Savitar Series:
Journey's End
Savitar
Confluence
Savitar Series Collection

Bram Nielson Series
The Fold
The Message
Fold Wormhole
Negative Fold
Ripples in Time
Bram Nielson Collection

Single Science Fiction Books:
Current Past and Future
The Event
The Door
Viajante 7

Characters in the Story

Alex	Cathy	Evercrest	Police Detective
Matthew	Timothy	Knolton	Alex's suitor
Rose-Anne	Germain	Evercrest	Alex's mother
Russel	Johnson	Evercrest	Alex's father
Helping Hands charity			Alex's nonprofit org
Trey		McGregor	Alex's Detective Partner
Lindsey		McGregor	Wife
Nolan		McGregor	Son
Johnnie		Smith	Old Viet Vet
Mary		Higgins	Johnnie's Phili "friend"
Bruce	Lincoln	Johnson	Cinci Chief of Detectives
Mary-Anne	Leslie	Johnson	Chiefs Wife
Bill	Hamilton	Danson	Detective
Travis	Bailey	Carter	Detective
Dr. Rogers			Coroner
Jane	Elousie	Stradford	Lieutenant Governor
Felix			Proprietor fishing dock
Golden Goose			Name of the Yacht
Sandra		Olson	Policewoman guard
Annie	Lorie	Scots	Missing girl
Linda		Annies	older daughter
Lorie		Annies	second daughter
Harold		Zimmerman	Chicago DEA
James	Oscor	Kaizer	Sheriff of Wiggin
Abbie	Alisa	Bender	protect Alex married James
John	S.	Williams	Lawyer that was abused
Hanna		Waverly	John's mate
Angelica			Angel on the hill
Brian		Lexter	Cinci FBI Bureau Chief
Cais		Leu	Alex's Viet friend
Tracy		Hunter	Trey's Analyst
Lissa		Maliber	Mother of missing son

Jesse	T	Maliber	Lissa's son
April		Maliber	Lissa's Daughter
Rick			Bully Leader
Eli			Bully
Sylvester			Bully

www.remwriter95.net/

Published by: Around the World Publishing LLC.

www.ingramcontent.com/pod-product-compliance
Lightning Source LLC
Chambersburg PA
CBHW070549100726
47907CB00004B/1320